Starchsers:

The Stars Will Rise

By Kay Hawkins

Starchasers: The Stars Will Rise

Kay Hawkins

Published by Kay Hawkins

Copyright 2017

First Edition

ISBN:   978-0-9959794-0-6

Dedication

To Dirk Benedict & Richard Hatch
I would not be here today if it wasn't for them
RIP Richard
Sorry you never got the to see the book in print

Chapter 1


Skyler made his way through the courtyard of the United Galactic Forces. He scanned the grounds and the tall buildings. There were old brick barracks next to tall steel towers.

He stretched his neck up, his face beaming with joy. "So this is the United Galactic Force's Academy. These next four years are going to be easy."

A group of other cadets were passing by. One of them overheard Skyler's remark. "It's seven, you idiot!"

Skyler brushed off the comment and kept enjoying the view. I am finally here. He glanced at the newsletter that was open on his issued tablet. It read 'Orientation for new cadets 10 a.m. in the main hall auditorium.'

He made it to the main hall and through the corridor. He took his time to admire the architecture while trying not to get in anyone's way. This was the moment he had waited for his entire life, a dream come true. Nothing was going to stop him now. With his head in the clouds, he bumped into a cadet, losing his balance.

He was a taller, older male. At first glance, he could pass for a human, but his eyes were too wide and their color didn't appear natural. The top of his ears looked like they had been cut off, and his nose was straighter than any other man's was, occupying more space on his face than Skyler would expect. They stared at each other, neither one admitting fault.

"Watch where you're going, you Electric Bug," Skyler said.

The older cadet glared. "Quite an ignorant mouth you got on you, White Meat."

They both scowled at one another as an announcement blared through the speaker system. "Orientation is starting in twenty minutes. Please make your way to the auditorium."

Skyler paused, shrugged and continued his path into the auditorium. Once inside he began his search to find a seat.

Jackpot. There was an empty seat beside an attractive blonde female cadet. He swiftly made his way over and snagged the seat and sat down.

"Hello there, I see you're new. How about after this we help each other find our rooms?"

Her face turned beet red from his comment. "I'm sorry. I'm already seeing someone. He's a third year, so I know my way around, thank you."

He brushed his honey blonde hair back and checked around for another seat. He spotted another one next to a cute red-haired girl a few rows away. Before he could move from where he was, the lights dimmed. He was out of time. He had no choice but to take a seat next to the girl who had rejected him.

There was a mix of the commodores and admirals on stage in full dress uniform, sitting in rows of fold out chairs. The three fleet admirals stood out from the rest, regal in their golden uniforms. These were the heads of the entire United Galactic Forces. Their multicolored mandarin collar jackets, and neatly pressed matching pants for the men and skirts for the women, mesmerized Skyler. Blue for engineering, maroon for medical, orange for science, grey for ground, black for security, and green for command.

He dreamed of being a captain one day. Maybe, far in his future, he would even be an admiral.

The speeches on stage continued. He tried to stay focused, but his eyes were too heavy. He soon gave in, closed his eyes and he drifted off to sleep.

Two hours passed, and the speeches were just about finished. He awoke and brushed back his hair, just in time to hear the end of Fleet Admiral Cane's speech. "… As you begin your journey, young cadets, take these two pieces of advice with you. Look behind you before you make any decisions and Iter sicut stellas: travel like the stars."

When the lights came back on, everyone stood up and applauded before they made their way out of the auditorium.

On his way out, he saw a fine young female brunette cadet walking with her equally sexy blonde friend. He strolled between them and introduced himself. "Hi ladies. I'm Cadet Therris, but you lovelies can call me Skyler."

The girls blushed, and the brunette introduced herself. "My name is Devina, and my friend here is Amelia. It's nice to meet you too, Skyler."

With a simple smirk, he turned on his charming smile. He ambled with them. "So, ladies, are you two single? If so, how would you like to come on over to my room and we can have a private cadet orientation?"

The girls both giggled. Devina batted her long eyelashes at Skyler. "First day and you're trying to pick us up? Are you sure you're safe?"

Skyler wiggled his eyebrows. "Ladies, I am always safe. I'm only asking for an hour of your time. You have fun, I have a good time, and we all walk away happy. How about it? Let's make this first day of the rest of our lives memorable."

The two girls stepped aside and whispered to one another. Amelia focused her attention back to Skyler and shot him a smile. "You got yourself a deal."

Skyler grinned. He gave each girl a kiss on the cheek before showing them to his dorm room. Once outside the dorm room, Skyler and the girls lingered in front of his door. He took turns kissing them and rubbing the upper parts of their bodies. He opened the door to his room. He leaned Amelia against the doorway, kissing her neck and rubbing her hips. Devina kissed Skyler's neck and reached around to unzip his cadet uniform jacket.

They all heard a loud cough come from inside the room. They stopped what they were doing. Skyler noticed a pale blue alien with pastel green puff ball hair glaring right at them.

Skyler lifted his face, covered in lipstick. "Oh, hello there. Are you my roommate?"

The alien picked his suitcase up off the bed while glowering at him. "Yes, I am, but I'm not staying. There seems to be a mistake in my file."

With his hands on the small of their backs, Skyler led the girls over to his bed on the left side of the sky blue standard room. The girls perched on the bed. "Oh, really? I'm sorry to hear that. I hope they work things out for you."

The pale blue alien stalked across the room with his suitcase in hand. He gave Skyler and the girls one last glare before departing. "They will."

Skyler did not pay any attention to the alien and carried on with the girls. He shifted to his right and leaned Devina on the bed, kissing her neck and unzipping her top. Amelia seemed to have noticed the alien's glare. "Why do you think he was so upset?"

Skyler had his face between her friend's breasts. He lifted his head. "Who cares? This means we have more privacy."

Skyler was moaning with pleasure and delight until a familiar face entered the small two single bed dorm room.

He looked up from the bed. "If it isn't the Electric Bug. Want one of the girls?"

The alien with docked-like ears shook his head. "With an attitude like that, it's no wonder the other guy left."

He lowered his brow and continued. "Lucky for him, he did have the wrong room and I'm your new roommate. When you were in high school, did you ever go to your alien edict class, by any chance?"

Skyler gave his new roommate a puzzled expression. "Uh, I don't think my school offered that class?"

The man smacked his forehead. "Well then, just so you know, the other guy was a Modorlean. His race is extremely modest, and even the slightest sign of public affection makes them uncomfortable."

Skyler pulled back the covers a bit to reveal the girls. "And this doesn't make you uncomfortable. Right, Buggy?"

Amelia quickly grabbed the covers and pulled them back down. While Devina just laughed.

The man cringed, turning away from the girls and his naked roommate. "My name is Michael M. Jones. I am a third-year cadet. I am not a bug, I am a Squallite, but you're just a human. And I don't want to see that."

He signaled the girls to stop. He rolled over to check Michael out. "You're an Alien with a human name. How does that work, don't you have names like Zaphod and Xeenon?"

He paused and stared at the girls. "Wait, don't answer that, these girls have a job to finish, and they have been waiting long enough."

Michael rolled his eyes as Skyler continued his job under the sheets. Skyler could hear Michael's footsteps leave the room.

\*\*\*

Michael sat on the cold marble floor of the hall and waited for a sign to tell him it was safe to go back in. He scanned the hallway. I can't be the only cadet who was kicked out of their room.

While he waited there, searing pain shot through his head. A loud noise and announcement came blaring through the speakers. Michael jerked his attention to the PA speaker system on the ceiling.

"All cadets must evacuate the building! This is not a drill! Please exit out of the closest door and head to the north building. Fourth year and higher, report to the hangar for duty. There is an attack on the base. Repeat, there is an attack on the base!"

Michael scrambled to his feet and shoved open the door to the dorm.

Skyler jumped out of bed, struggling to put on his pants. "What's this all about?"

The girls hopped off the bed. They retrieved their clothes off the floor and quickly got dressed.

Michael charged into the room, peered out the window between the two beds and pointed. "That's what's going on."

A large alien fighter shot around the base, the courtyard and some of the other buildings. All of them watched in horror until a friendly fighter hit it knocking out one of its engines causing it the engine explode.

They rushed out of the building. Skyler and Michael parted ways from the girls. Once outside, they raced towards the crash site and observed an oddly familiar alien running from the site towards the hangar.

Michael pulled out his camera and began taking pictures as they ran. Hopefully I can get a good shot of the crash.

Instinctively, Michael ran after Skyler, who had his eyes on the alien in the distance. The hangar began to go into emergency lockdown, but it was too late. The alien made it in.

Michael caught a glimpse of the team of security officers who were also rushing after the alien. The emergency hangar door was four feet from closing. Before the gate closed, they managed to slide in under the door. The security officers were stuck on the outside. The two boys didn't stop and continued to run after the alien. The alien rushed to one of the older unused parts of the hangar.

They saw the alien climbing into an old shuttlecraft. Skyler ran and jumped into the shuttle. He grabbed the alien, punched him without watching his fist, and cut his knuckle on the crown of the horns growing out of the creature's forehead. He glared at the alien. He had rough skin like tree bark, sharp pointed teeth and small thorny horns coming out of his forehead and around his head, like a crown. Skyler backed away.

Michael tried to get to them.

He yelled to Skyler, "What's taking you so long? He's going to get away!"

Skyler raised his cut right hand to punch his assailant one more time. The alien stretched out his long-clawed hand and pushed Skyler out of the shuttle, closed the door and flew off.

Michael watched Skyler falling and caught him before he hit the concrete floor. Michael helped Skyler to his feet. "Are you all right?"

Skyler straightened his uniform and examined his bleeding hand. "He cut my hand."

Michael bit his lip. He pulled a roll of bandages out of his pocket. He held Skyler's hand and wrapped it up. "That should hold until we get you to a doctor."

Michael finished bandaging up the hand. He picked up his head and glanced around the old hangar, a place full of history and sadness. These parts were once ships and shuttlecrafts. Now they were a junk heap, parts of history outdated and no longer in use, and tossed aside since they were considered inoperable or obsolete.

Michael peered at the junk heap he had seen too many times. He noticed Skyler was distracted by the sights.

He heard a click in the background. Oh, right, the lockdown. The security team will be here the second they release it.

He searched around and noticed a vent. He tugged Skyler's arm and pulled him into the ventilation system. "Come on, we have to get this information to Fleet Admiral Cane."

Skyler followed Michael through the vent and out of the hangar. He noticed that as soon as they got out of there, lockdown lifted, and all the security officers rushed into the building, towards Fleet Admiral Cane's office.

Once they were at the office, there was chaos everywhere. The phones were ringing off the hook. People were running back and forth with stacks of papers. Michael and Skyler tried to waltz into the fleet admiral's office.

The secretary shouted at them as they headed towards the door. She got up and stopped them. "Hey, you boys can't go in. The fleet admiral is very busy, and he's not seeing anyone!"

Michael retorted. "Listen, we have info on the attack. We need to talk to Fleet Admiral Cane now."

The secretary glared at them. "I cannot let you boys in there."

Skyler glanced at the secretary's nameplate. "Celia, please, page the fleet admiral and tell him Skyler Therris needs to see him now!"

She hesitantly hit the intercom button on the wall and buzzed the fleet admiral. They could hear papers rustling and a phone dropping. The secretary spoke into the speaker. "Sir, there are two cadets here, a Therris and one's a Squallite. They say they have info on the attack and would like to speak with you."

The secretary didn't even have to tell them. The boys had already bolted into the office.

Cane's face lit up when he saw Skyler. He brushed his frosted brown hair back in an attempt to fix it. There were stacks of unsorted papers buried his desk, and Half a bottle of brandy sat on the desk. His one eye was bloodshot and sunken in, his other eye covered by an eye patch. He tried to put on a good face for the boys. "Ah, Cadet Therris and Jones. Nice to see you boys. What is this info you have?"

Skyler spoke up. "Well, sir, we charged after the guy, and he was this weird horned alien with tan skin and sharp claws. We made it into the hangar where he stole a shuttle. I tried to fight him off; I punched him, and his horns cut my hand."

He held out his bandaged hand to show Cane.

The fleet admiral unwrapped the bandage and examined the long cut across Skyler's knuckle.

"So the Cass are at it again," he mumbled to himself.

Michael got his camera ready and moved closer to the desk. He activated the camera and brought up the pictures. "See, Fleet Admiral, these are the photos of the wreckage." He zoomed in. "I also got a clear shot of the guy who did it."

The fleet admiral switched his focus away from Skyler's hand and glanced over the pictures. "Excellent pictures, Cadet Jones. May I borrow your camera for evidence? I promise you it will be returned."

Michael handed him the camera. "Here you are, it's yours."

Fleet Admiral Cane pocketed the camera. "Thank you, Cadet Jones. Skyler, see a doctor about that wound. It looks pretty deep."

"Yes, sir." He made his way towards the door with Michael.

Cane bit his lip. "Stay safe, you two."

They got out of the office and headed towards the clinic.

Michael glanced at Skyler. "How come the fleet admiral called you Skyler back there and not Cadet Therris?"

Skyler rubbed his arm. "Beats me."


Chapter 2


Michael grabbed the letter posted on the outside of the door as he entered the room. He was returning after his morning shower at the end of the hall.

Skyler was sitting on the bed in his underwear, examining the wound on his hand.

"How's the hand healing? Looks like it will leave a nice scar," Michael commented.

Skyler raised his head away from his hand and towards Michael. "Not sure yet, would be cool if it did. It's only been a few weeks, but it still hurts. My fever broke last night. The infection must be gone."

Michael held out the letter. "Hey, Skyler, did you see that we had a letter on the door?"

Skyler shifted forward. "Oh, maybe it's from one of the hot girls we saw at the bar. I told you one was eyeing you. You should've joined us in the back room."

Michael cringed at the comment. He opened the letter. "No, it's not, and that's the last time I go drinking with you." He skimmed the letter. "It says here that we are being honored at an award ceremony for our bravery during the attack. Holy fudge nuggets! Do you know what this means, Skyler?"

"Yup, one month here and I get a medal. Chicks will be all over that." He leaned back with a sly smile.

Michael scrunched his face at Skyler, shaking his head.

Skyler leaned closer, craning his neck to read the letter. "So when is the ceremony? I hope it's before the weekend."

Michael tossed the letter at Skyler and rolled his eyes. "Here, you find out the details since this doesn't seem to mean the same to you as it does to me."

Skyler snatched the letter. He grinned with anticipation. "Friday after school sounds good to me." He glanced over at Michael. "But what does this mean to you?"

Michael was taken aback. Why would Skyler ask or even care? "What does it matter to you? You never care about anything I have to say."

Skyler rolled his shoulders. "I don't care, you mentioned it."

A knock came from the door. Skyler called out, "Come in!"

A girl with long blonde hair and a curvaceous figure peeked in. "Hey, Skyler, want to meet up after classes today?"

Skyler grinned and brushed back his hair, putting on his winning smile "You bet, see you later."

The girl licked her lips and left the room.

Michael put on his cadet jacket. "Speaking of classes, we need to get going."

Skyler rolled his eyes. "Yes, class. I don't mind it, but do we have to do this whole buddy system thing?"

Michael zipped his blue cadet jacket and waited for Skyler to finish putting on his forest green cadet uniform. "I like this buddy system as much as you, but it's for safety after the attack. It won't last much longer once the whole terrorist hype calms down."

Once Skyler had finished putting on his uniform, he followed Michael out of the room. Michael checked his watch. "We're running a bit late, thanks to you. We are going to have to rush to get to class."

The boys hurried through the halls. If they happened to be lucky, they would make it right when the doors closed for Skyler's class. When they were less than ten feet away, the bell rang, and the doors locked. No chance of getting into anyone's class now.

"Dammit, this sucks! What am I supposed to do now?" Skyler hit his head against the stone wall.

Michael searched around. He seized Skyler's hand. "Come on, follow me."

He dragged him to the janitor's closet next to the class. He opened the door and stretched up and opened the vent. "This vent will take us into the class. We can listen in this way. It's a cooling vent, so we don't have to worry about the temperature."

Skyler's hands were shaking. "Isn't it a bit small?"

Michael examined the size. "I think you should fit. If not, I will find you another way. Come on, I'll help you up."

Skyler managed to gather the courage to try to reach up and squeeze himself into the vent, but his sweaty palms wouldn't hold.

Michael cupped his hands to offer a boost and leaned down.

Skyler stepped in Michael's hands. When he made it into the vent, he noticed that it was bigger on the inside. He struggled to pull himself up. Once he was halfway in, he wiggled his hips and managed a military crawl. Michael squeezed himself in. Being much taller than Skyler, he didn't need a boost. Michael's limber Squallite body had no problem climbing and crawling through the vent. "Keep going, Skyler, the class should be about another five feet. You should see the screen coming up."

Skyler kept moving, and the vent opened further. He saw the screen and shifted around so he could sit more comfortably in the vent. Michael moved next to Skyler.

"Thanks, but how did you know about the vent?"

Michael touched his chin. "You know what I am, but how much do you know about Squallites?"

Skyler held up his fingers, counting. "I know they chew on wires, fix ships and have orange eyes, unlike yours. Yours are different. They're like bugs or something."

Michael cringed at the comment. "You little prick, I wear blue contacts, and we don't eat wires, we hear electric waves. We also know where the wires need fixing. We have limber bodies so we can get into tight spots, and we're more like earth rodents than bugs. That's the basics."

Skyler listened, thoughtful. "So, if you're an alien why are you my roommate? I didn't think they mixed aliens with the humans."

Michael held back the urge to hurt Skyler. "This is a multicultural space academy. The Human Prick Academy is across the street. You might have had your name on the wrong list."

Skyler rolled his eyes. "Very funny, Mr. Rat. I just meant that if Squallites are seen as lesser than humans why would they mix us and not segregate?"

Michael snarled at Skyler. "I didn't realize that you were such a racist. We are not though. Humans think we are because of our pacifist nature. Society is changing. There were things we used to be excluded from before, but now we're not. But you're lucky you can be a captain. We are still only allowed in the Engineering Division."

Skyler widened his eyes at Michael. "I didn't realize I was offensive. I wasn't trying to be. I was raised with humans, no aliens around. So I don't know how to deal with them."

"If I had just met you, I would believe you, but I have seen how you act around the female aliens."

Skyler scratched his head and laughed. "Ya, well, they're hot, so I treat them like I would any other beautiful lady I meet."

Michael forced a laugh. "See, that is what I mean. If you can treat the female aliens with equality, then why not the men?"

Skyler paused for a minute. "I can think of a few reasons." He chuckled.

They heard a bang on the door of the vent.

Michael jumped away from the opening of the vent. The teacher called out, "Cadet Therris, I'm not sure who you are talking to, but listening in the vent shows the effort that you want to learn. But if you keep talking to your friend through my class, I will have you thrown out. For the rest of the year. So be quiet."

Skyler covered his mouth. "Yes, ma'am, sorry. I won't talk the rest of class."

The teacher returned to the front of the class and continued the lesson.

Michael slowly moved back towards the opening of the vent. "Sorry about getting you in trouble."

"Don't sweat it. Come on, let's listen."

At the end of class, Skyler and Michael emerged from the vent and made it to their next class.

\*\*\*

At the end of the day, after all their classes finished, the boys headed back to the room. Skyler changed out of his uniform and into a tight black t-shirt and tight blue jeans. He put his uniform on the hanger and placed it in their shared closet.

Michael changed out of his uniform as well. He took advantage of the shared desk between their beds to do his work.

Skyler smirked, checking his blue jeans for his wallet. "So you sure you don't want to come to the bar with me tonight? I'll probably be back late."

Michael drew out his digital notebook. "You go out and have fun. I need to get some homework done, which is really what you should be doing. By the way, can I borrow your textbooks?"

Skyler ambled over to the full-length mirror to comb his hair. "You don't know what you're missing, but sure you can. I've got to make them look a little used this year."

Soon the blonde girl came to the door. "Hey, Skyler, you ready to go and have some fun tonight?"

Skyler donned his winning smile and strolled over to the door, edging closer to the girl. "I'm ready and waiting."

Skyler kissed the girl passionately on the lips and placed his hand on her hips. Together they rubbed their hands over each other's bodies and kissed like hungry wolves.

Michael had his head aimed away from them but could hear them. "Please, you two should leave now."

Skyler and the girl stopped and peered in Michael's direction and laughed. "Suit yourself. Party pooper."

Michael let out a big groan and shouted, "Whatever. Get out!"

Skyler and the girl took off in their matching leather jackets.

Finally, they're gone. Now I get some well-needed peace and relaxation. This was what he had been waiting for since the beginning of the year. The room was quiet, and he was alone, a perfect time to study. He sat at the desk and tried to focus on his books, but for some reason couldn't. There was something missing. The room was almost…

"No, no!" Michael shouted out of frustration into the quiet room. "No. I can't stand the guy, and when he finally leaves, I want him here? He is a little prick, why should I even care where he is? Why do I want him here? Why, Skyler, do you have to drive me nuts? Even when you're not here."

"Ok, this isn't working."

He put his books away and laid down on his bed. He stretched out. Crossing his arms, he tried to meditate. Something was missing. There was no noise. How was he to meditate in such silence?

Michael rose from the bed. He had never touched Skyler's stuff without permission before, but this was a mission for sanity. He nervously crossed onto Skyler's side of the room, picked up and switched on Skyler's antique boom box, and put in one of Skyler's Bryan Adams CDs. It wasn't the best replacement for Skyler, but it would do until the bar closed. Michael laid back on the bed, finally able to close his eyes.

Skyler got in close to four in the morning. He brought back a different girl from the one he had left with earlier. This one was a redhead. He got to the room and heard his music playing. Michael was now fast asleep. He chuckled to himself and continued with the girl.

## Chapter 3

Michael awoke later than normal, opened his eyes and saw Skyler already dressed and ready for class. Michael's eyes were red and bloodshot, he tried to get up.

Skyler combed his hair in the mirror and checked over his shoulder. "It's about time you woke up, sleepy head. You were asleep when I got back, and I would think you would have been better rested."

Michael stumbled out of bed and put on his uniform. "I tried to sleep, but I couldn't seem to, so I didn't get as much as it seems."

Skyler slid his comb in his pocket and turned around to face Michael. "It seems I'm starting to rub off on you, I see." He pointed to his twentieth-century boom box.

Michael cringed as he slid on his jacket. "Don't say it like that. And sorry, I didn't mean to touch your stuff ..."

Skyler leaned on the end of his bed. "Don't worry, dude. But one question. There is a rumor going around saying that you're gay and have a crush on me. Is that true?"

Michael massaged his temples. "You're my roommate, I guess you should know. I'm straight, I admire but I am not attracted to you in that way."

Skyler smiled and rubbed his neck. "I can't argue with that statement."

Michael rolled his eyes. "Anyway, I don't like to talk about it, and my sexuality doesn't even matter. I can't have sex anyway."

Skyler narrowed his eyes. "What do you mean? Are you a eunuch or something?"

Michael sighed. "No, but I don't know who my mother is. She died in childbirth and my dad never told me about her. And in Squallite traditions, before you have sex both sides need to know your family history at least one generation back. And on top of that, I am Catholic so no sex before marriage. So, I suppress everything with meditation and try to perceive myself as asexual."

"Dude, that is so sad. Have you ever thought about talking to your dad about your mom?"

Michael shook his head. "It won't do any good. I have asked a few times, but he brushes it off. He is still too hurt."

"Right, okay. Well, as long as we are coming clean. I only like women. I think it's nice you admire me." Skyler scanned around the room. "Hey, do you know what time the ceremony is tonight? Because I've got to find my dress uniform and I haven't seen it since they issued them, before orientation."

Michael rubbed his forehead. "You can't use mine. I need it too. We can look around for it later. There will be time after class."

Skyler rummaged through the pile of clothes strewn across his side of the room.

Michael tried to open his eyes enough to put in his contacts but couldn't seem to get them in. Once he did manage to place them in, they burned, like pouring alcohol on an open wound. He placed the contacts on the desk. His eyes were too bloodshot to wear them today. A brief sadness came over him. He glimpsed the clock. They still had about fifteen minutes before they should leave for class. Hmm, I thought it was later. I guess I will help him.

"Found it!" Skyler called out from under his bed. "It got stuck between two of my boxes."

Michael focused his attention to across the room. He saw Skyler holding a wrinkled forest green satin jacket and the matching pants of his dress uniform. "I'm glad you found it, but how are we going to get it cleaned in time? Also, you should have it hung up and cleaned it a long time ago. Look at it. Have you ever even worn it yet?"

Skyler spread the uniform on the bed, rubbed his hands over it and tried to de-wrinkle it. "I have a social life. I don't have time, and I did wear it once. That was to see if it fit, which it does. I'm sorry we all can't be perfectionists like you."

*This is what I was missing last night? I must have gone insane or something.*

Skyler snapped his fingers. "Hey, there's a dry cleaner on campus for uniforms, let's go there before class. I bet it could be done by the end of the day."

Michael checked the clock, and they now had only ten minutes before they had to leave for class. "We don't have time, Skyler, we have to get to class."

Skyler sat down on his bed, cupping his hand on his chin, contemplating. "Then we'll be late for class. We'll run to the cleaners and then go into the vent. It worked yesterday."

Michael sighed. "That works for you, but what about me? You will get to class, but my class doesn't have a vent around it. Sure, I like going to your class, but that's two days in a row that I am missing mine."

Skyler paused. "Well then, we break the rules and split up. We leave the room together and run to class."

*I don't want to break rules, but it does sound like a good idea. But what if Skyler gets distracted?* Michael contemplated the two options. *What do I do? Leave Skyler behind and get to class or go* with Skyler and help him? He pondered the ideas in his mind while the first bell rang. Only one idea made sense.

"Come on, Skyler, let's get your uniform cleaned."

Michael headed towards the door.

Michael and Skyler rushed through the hall to the south end of the building. The dry cleaner was across the courtyard, beyond the barracks and in the same building as the main hall. When they got there, an older lady was working in the back, organizing the clothes on the racks.

Skyler dropped his uniform on the counter. "Can I get this cleaned for the end of the day? I have a ceremony to go to, and I really do need this cleaned."

The lady examined the uniform for wrinkles and a few stains. "Is five o'clock good for you?"

Skyler turned to Michael, who shook his head. "Five is cutting it close. Is there a way we can pick it up for, let's say, lunch time?"

The lady glanced in back to check the items waiting for cleaning. "Okay, I can do it, but it will cost you extra."

Michael frowned. "I thought this was a free dry cleaning service for officers and cadets?"

The lady frowned. "Yes, it is. But if your friend wants this big of a job done by noon, he is going to have to pay."

Skyler patted Michael on the back. "It's okay, I have money. As long as the job gets done I am fine."

Michael sighed and backed off.

Relieved the uniform would be taken care of, the boys headed out of the cleaners and towards their next class.

After the school day was over, Michael and Skyler journeyed back to the room to put on their uniforms, all freshly cleaned and pressed. Michael loved the cold watery silky touch of his dark blue satin fold-over jacket with gold piping and matching cotton wool pants.

Skyler slid his uniform out of the bag and examined it. "It's so clean, don't you think? And mmm, it's still a bit warm."

Michael combed his short brown hair to the side and tried putting in his contacts again. This time it worked.

He scrutinized Skyler's uniform. "Well, it has been cleaned, and you better take care of it from now on. Who knows how long it will be before you wear it again, so take better care of it."

Skyler changed into his uniform, which had the same design as Michael's but was in a forest green. "So what time do we have to be there?"

Michael finished with his hair and checked the letter. "Anytime now, so hurry up. We can't be late for this one."

Skyler finished with his uniform and quickly ran a comb through his hair to straighten his honey blond curls.

Once finished dressing they hurried to the auditorium. Michael searched for a sign to say where they were supposed to go. Fleet Admiral Cane approached them. "Good day, boys, I hope you are all ready, and it's nice to see you are on time. If you would care to follow me, I will show you to where you need to be."

They both followed the fleet admiral to the stage of the auditorium where there were five foldout chairs all lined up. Two for them. On the opposite side of the podium, there were some chairs set up for the fleet admirals. They sat in the chairs and waited for the ceremony. The crowd came, and the room filled up.

Michael spotted his father sitting in the front row. He was glad his dad came. He wanted to go over and talk to him before it started, but there wasn't time. The lights dimmed, and Fleet Admiral Cane stepped up to the podium. "My fellow officers and cadets: Today, we are here to honor five great people for being so helpful to the United Galactic Forces. These fine young people went out of their way to risk their lives to help us all in the most recent terrorist attacks and we're awarding them the medal of bravery. Now please give a round of applause for them."

The crowd clapped, and Michael's heart raced. He was so honored to be up there. One by one Fleet Admiral Cane called out the names of the people, who got up to receive their awards.

When it was Skyler's turn, he swaggered to the podium.

Cane smiled, pinned the medal on his jacket and whispered to Skyler, "Your father would be proud."

A brief sadness fell over Skyler. Quickly he covered his emotions with a smile. "Thank you, sir." He went back to his seat and waited for the ceremony to be over.

After the ceremony, Michael strode over to his father and embraced him. His dad, a taller version of his son, ruffled Michael's hair. "Congratulations, son. I am so proud of you."

Michael hugged his dad tighter, smiling. "Thank you, Dad, that means a lot to me."

They broke the hug.

Skyler walked over to Michael. "So you're Michael's dad?"

Michael's father smiled. "Yes, I'm Sam Jones, and you are Skyler Therris. I knew your father, he was a great man. I'm sure he would have been proud of you today."

Skyler's eyes lit up. "You knew my father?"

Sam smiled. "I wasn't a member of his crew, but I helped him out a few times, and he was a great man."

Skyler was left speechless, not sure how to respond. "Thank you, sir."

A silence fell over the three. Michael broke it. "Skyler is the roommate I told you about."

Michael's father studied Skyler and turned to his son. "I figured that. I'm glad you two are roommates. I wonder what the fleet admiral was thinking when he placed you boys together."

Michael was about to say something when Admiral Cane came up and chimed in, "You're talking about me? I hope it is all good, Commodore Jones."

Sam grinned. "Fleet Admiral Cane, it is nice to see you again. It has been a long time."

Fleet Admiral Cane grinned back. "It has been a little too long, and we should meet up sometime. I am tight for time right now. I came to return this to Cadet Jones."

The fleet admiral extracted a metallic red camera from his pocket and handed it to Michael. "Thank you, Cadet Jones, this was a huge help in the case."

Michael collected his camera. "Thank you, sir, I'm glad and always will be willing to help in any way I can."

The fleet admiral grinned. "We need more like you, Cadet Jones."

The two saluted, and the admiral turned to Skyler. "How's the hand healing, Cadet Therris?"

Skyler held up his hand and showed it to the admiral. "Don't need a bandage anymore. I got a few stitches, but it should be all healed soon."

The fleet admiral smiled. "I am glad to hear that, Skyler, and I hope all stays well. If you ever need to see me about anything, just stop by my office. If I am there, just walk in, and don't worry about the secretary."

"Thank you, sir."

Fleet Admiral Cane saluted Skyler and the rest of them and headed off.

Once again, it confused Michael why Cane treated Skyler so informally.

Skyler had an overbearing sense of pride come over him. "So Michael, want to go to the bar and get a few drinks in celebration?"

Michael had no intentions of going, even under the circumstances. "Listen, Skyler, I would love to, but I think I'd rather spend some time with my father."

Sam turned to his son. "Go, have fun with your friend. I always will be here. I want you to have fun, don't worry about me."

Michael didn't see any other options. Damn, now I have to go out with Skyler. He put on a nervous smile. "Whatever you say, Dad."

Skyler patted Michael on the back and grinned. "Great, we're going to have a wild night."

Michael chuckled nervously. "Come on, Skyler, let's get changed."

Skyler waved to Michael's dad. "It was nice to meet you, sir. Hope to see you again."

Sam waved back to them. "It was nice to meet you too, Skyler. Keep my son out of trouble."

Skyler laughed. "I can't guarantee his safety."

Michael quickly steered Skyler away. They headed back to their room to change into their casual clothes.

Skyler put on his tight leather girl-getting pants and fixed his hair.

"You ready to party?" Skyler asked.

Michael rolled his eyes. "We're not going to party that much."

Skyler flung his comb onto his unmade bed. "Ya, keep telling yourself that."

They took off to the campus bar. It was in walking distance on the outskirts of the academy.

Once they arrived, Skyler waved to the bartender and signaled for two beers. "So, Michael, see anyone you're interested in here tonight?"

The waitress came buy with their two beers.

"I came here to celebrate. You might be here for action, but not me. Now, let's toast." Michael held up his beer.

Skyler clinked his beer with Michael's.

"To bravery and good times," Skyler said.

As Skyler toasted, he noticed a girl from across the room; a gorgeous strawberry blonde cadet with a natural set of cat ears standing at the end of the bar. She had a perfect hourglass figure. He smiled when he spotted her cute small round bottom sticking out as she leaned against the bar counter and waited for her drinks.

Skyler sipped his beer and clambered up out of his chair. "Hey, Michael, see you in a bit. There is someone I've got to talk to."

Michael swiveled to watch where Skyler was going. He too noticed the lovely strawberry blonde. I've got to go and talk to her. Skyler is just going to screw this up. While Skyler was ogling the girl, Michael spotted a big burly guy barreling towards his roommate. Michael tried to get there before Skyler did.

It was too late and the man purposely bumped into Skyler. "You were the guy who was with my Sheila yesterday?"

Shit, I knew this would happen eventually. Michael stood next to Skyler. "No, he wasn't. He was with me the entire night, we were studying."

The man glared at Michael. "Is that so? Then why does this punk match the description of the guy my girl was with last night?"

Before Michael could respond, Skyler butted in. "You must not be a good boyfriend if your girl is running around on you."

Shock and fear shot through Michael when he observed the guy's eyes glow red with anger. The man, who was twice his size, raised his fist. "What did you say, you little punk?"

Michael moved between them. "Listen, I think what he was saying is this negative attitude here is not attractive, and it will scare any women away. I assure you, my friend has nothing to do with your girlfriend."

Michael had no idea why he was standing up for Skyler. He knew his roommate was guilty.

The guy's face burned with rage. "Listen to me, Mr. Rat. Get out of the way because I know what this punk did to my girlfriend, and he is going to pay for it."

Michael's blood boiled. "I tried to be nice to you, but you're the one who doesn't want to play fair."

The guy shoved Michael out of the way. "Stay out of this."

Skyler put on a nervous smile. "Hey, dude, I don't want to get into anything. I think you need to relax."

The guy's rage grew. "No one tells me what to do, and no one touches my girlfriend but me."

He raised his fist and punched Skyler in the jaw, knocking him onto a table.

Michael swung at the guy, aiming for his jaw and getting his chest. The guy's friends bolted from their chairs and lined up behind their friend.

Skyler got back up and punched the guy in the stomach.

Michael could tell they were outnumbered, but he wasn't going down without a fight. They all began throwing punches left, right and center. He caught sight of the big guy using Skyler as a punching bag. Michael kept throwing the punches, but they were still no closer to winning.

The bouncer at the bar came over to them, got rid of the big guys and told Michael and Skyler to get out. They showed themselves out with wounds on their faces.

Once back in their room Michael pulled out his first aid kit and helped Skyler clean up his wounds. "You took quite a beating back there. Are you sure you are going to be okay?"

Skyler winced in pain as he rubbed his swollen jaw. "Yeah, I should be fine once the swelling goes down. Good thing tomorrow is Saturday. I don't have to worry about going to class with a black eye."

Michael capped the Neosporin and closed his first aid kit. "I guess that's the only positive. Oh, and if you ever tell my dad about tonight, don't mention the fight."

Skyler choked back a laugh. "Okay, but you have to tell him I got lucky."

Michael tried to laugh too, but his sore jaw wouldn't let him. "Okay. Sounds like a fair trade."

Skyler released a deep breath. "You want to know the worst part about tonight? I didn't get to say hi to that cute redhead with the cat ears. I wonder what her name is?"

Michael had seen the girl around the academy before. He found her stunning, but never had the courage to talk to her.

I'm not going to say it, but that's was one girl I wish Skyler would've talked too.


Chapter 4

Weeks passed and the middle of the semester was coming up. Not much was going on, it was much of the same. Skyler had been with numerous girls in that time, but none were the strawberry blonde with light pink ears. She was still on his mind; he wanted her. She had to be a cadet, too, but where was she?

The door opened and Michael walked in. "Hey, Skyler, good news. I got us booked for study hall. We are going every Wednesday after class."

Skyler was sitting on his bed playing on his tablet. He looked up to respond to Michael. "Really, why did you pick Wednesday? Don't you know that's hump day, and you know what I like to do on hump day."

Exasperated, Michael strode over to the desk and searched for his notebooks. "Every day is hump day for you. If not Wednesday, what is a good day for you?"

Skyler flipped through his little black schedule book. "Third Sunday of November. That's a great day for study hall."

Michael closed his eyes and tried to imagine he was somewhere else. He rolled his eyes. "No, that will not work. Listen, you need to get off your ass and study, or you will fail the exams when it's time to take them."

Skyler pondered that advice. "But the exams are, like, months away. Why study now?"

Michael sighed, getting up from the desk chair. "Fine, don't go, but I have the time booked. It's your choice."

Skyler continued to ignore Michael and fixed his hair. He flipped through his little black book, trying to decide who he should call.

\*\*\*

After Michael finished his classes on Wednesday, he had troubles on his mind, like school and keeping up his grades. He was already third in his class, but he could've been doing better. He loved that he had a command division cadet as his roommate. He always wanted to be a captain, but because of his race, he would never be allowed. This way he could use Skyler's books and notes to study. So he was falling behind because he was doing the work of two people, even if he wasn't going to get credit for his work. He would rather have the skills than lose the chance ever to gain them.

He stopped by Skyler's class to pick him up. He was getting used to this buddy system now. He got to class, and Skyler was waiting. "So you want to go to study hall or not?"

Skyler stood outside of his classroom. "You know, I thought of it a few times today during my classes, but with my grades, I don't believe I need to."

Michael opened his mouth to argue and then he got another idea. "You do know there will be a lot of hot girls in study hall because girls love to hang out at the library."

Skyler's eyes brightened. "You don't say. In that case, I can't see why I wouldn't want to try it at least once."

Michael accepted it as a small victory.

They made their way to the library. They signed into study hall on the digital clipboard. There were lots of people there. Michael watched Skyler put on his charm as he sat next to some girls. Without any books, he leaned over towards the girls. "Hey, ladies, how about we take a break from studying and go out to the pub and see where it goes from there?"

The girls laughed at Skyler and one of them said, "Sorry, we're not interested." They got out of their chairs and moved to another table.

Skyler brushed it off and sat scoping the room for another attractive girl to pick up.

Michael brushed by Skyler and handed him a book. "At least look like you are planning to study."

Skyler accepted the book. Michael walked around, finding the textbooks they would both need.

***

Skyler didn't even glance at the cover of the book in his hand. He got up and circled around, scanning the room as he tried to find another girl. He spotted one from a distance and flirted with his eyes. She gave him a rude gesture.

Why did I listen to Michael?

Suddenly she appeared out of nowhere, the strawberry blonde from the bar. She had, at that moment, signed into study hall. This time, Skyler was not going to let her get away. He waited until she found a seat. Good, she's alone. Watching her sit on the other side of the room at an empty table, he swaggered over and made his move.

"Hello there. Is this seat taken?" He didn't wait for an answer. He sank down with his book. She smiled and read the title. "Chase Your Dreams, Not Tail: A Guide to Staying Focused." She laughed. "That's an interesting book to read in study hall."

He squinted at the cover. Coughing, he tossed the book onto another table. "That's not my book. That was for a friend. Hi, my name's Skyler Therris, and may I say how lovely you are."

She was still smiling. "Well, it's nice to meet you, but you know it's pretty lame for a guy as good looking as you to be picking girls up in study hall, right?"

He ran his fingers through his hair. "Yes, well, a guy's got to have options. Some are better than others, and from the looks of you and your golden eyes, I say this is a good one."

She rolled those golden eyes. "Right. Because if you're not here, you're at bars picking up other guy's girlfriends."

Heat flooded into Skyler's face, and he glanced away so she wouldn't notice. "The story is that the night before she came to me for help to get away from her mean boyfriend. I was only attempting to help, not steal her away."

***

Michael peered over at Skyler and saw he was with the cute redhead. Determined not to let Skyler scare this one away, he grabbed one last book he needed off the shelf and walked over to the table. He plopped the books on the table and he sat on the other side, across from them. Skyler had just finished explaining he wasn't the bad guy in the bar fight.

Michael tried some charm of his own. "That's what he says, but I know the truth, and I think you're intelligent enough to know it too."

She studied Michael who was kind enough to have removed Skyler's hand off her shoulder. "Hello, there. You his friend?"

Michael laughed. "More like an unfortunate roommate. Name's Michael Jones. I'm a third year."

He held out his hand. She shook it. "It's nice to meet you. I'm Kax Tillion, second year."

Michael slid a book over to Skyler to get him to shut up.

She smiled at Michael. "So, let me guess. You're the one who dragged him here?"

Michael laughed, admiring her royal purple uniform, and spotted a winged gold pin on her top. "Let's just say he owed me. Are you training to be a pilot?"

She grinned and placed her thumb under it to show Michael her pin. "That's what this means, and I can guess by your uniforms, you're an engineer and your friend wants to be a captain."

Skyler's face lit up. "You mean will be a captain, I won't settle for anything less."

She turned to Skyler. "I see. Well, I like a man who knows what he wants."

Michael butted in. "Pilot. That's a particularly hard division to be in. Isn't it true that if your coordinates are off by a small degree, you can end up in the sun?"

She turned back to Michael. "Yes. That's right, but my mom was a pilot, and I want to continue the legacy. And I love it."

Michael was impressed now. "That is very nice. But aren't you worried about dying?"

She grinned and her ears wiggled. "Someone has to do it until they improve the system, and it's what I love. Who wouldn't die for what they love?"

Her determination mesmerized Michael. "You sound wonderful–"

Skyler cut in, "So, you two want to get a few drinks after study hall or do you want to leave right now?"

Michael sighed and vacated his chair. "I guess now, since I don't think we will be getting much studying done at this rate."

Kax considered Skyler's offer. "I'll go only because Michael is joining us."

In Skyler's mind, evidently, all he heard was yes. "You got yourself a deal."

\*\*\*

Skyler and Michael were in the lunch hall. Skyler had been walking on air for the past week.

Michael narrowed his eyes at Skyler. "Why have you been so happy? I know you haven't slept with her yet."

Grabbing a plate of food, Skyler snickered. "I know, I can't even get her interested, but something about her makes me... Oh, I'll get her one day."

"Whatever you say. Come on, let's hurry up, get our lunch and sit down. I'm starving. I missed breakfast again because of you."

Skyler finished getting his food. In the distance, he spotted Kax eating by herself and headed over to see her.

Michael followed Skyler and took a seat across from Kax.

Skyler sat next to Kax. He noticed she was reading a textbook while trying to eat. "You know, it's lunchtime. No textbooks allowed."

With a smirk, Kax closed her book. "Ok, then let's play it your way."

"So, Kax, how's the studying going?" Michael picked up her textbook.

"Really good, haven't failed a test yet."

Skyler scoffed. "Well, you can't. I mean, am I right? For pilots, if you fail a test, you're out?"

She shook her head. "No, that's not all true. Exams yes, tests no. As long as you are not flying a craft, then you are safe."

"Interesting, I knew it was something like that." Michael flipped through the pages of the textbook.

Kax had been playing with her food. "I am also doing command classes, so that's something to fall back on. You're not in a second division, are you?"

Michael lowered the book. "No, I want to be a captain, but until they give Squallites equal rights, I can't. But I'm just an engineer, so I only took one division."

Skyler interrupted, "I'm only in command. I want to be a captain, nothing else, so why should I try to learn other skills?"

She shifted away. "You guys are a funny bunch. I was just about done when you came. I was about to clean up my tray and leave." She picked up her tray and rose from her seat.

Shit, she's leaving,

In a panic, Skyler clutched her arm. "Come on, you have half a sandwich left. Enjoy lunch with us, I won't bite."

She fidgeted with the tray in her hands. "Nothing personal. I don't have many friends, and I don't know how to deal with new people."

Michael extended a hand over the table and swatted Skyler's shoulder. "You just proved you don't. Keep your hands to yourself."

He relaxed his hand and let go. "I'm sorry, I shouldn't have grabbed your arm. I like you and I would like for you to give me another chance." He gave her his puppy dog eyes.

Kax let out a long sigh. "Skyler, you are a nice guy, but keep your hands to yourself."

"Skyler means no harm, he was just born with too much testosterone. I, on the other hand, will always respect your boundaries." Michael added.

Skyler focused on eating his lunch. His brow furrowed. Every time I make a move on this girl, she shuts me down, but Michael does that, and she likes him. I need to get rid of Michael. Then she will want me.

She gazed straight ahead at Michael. "If you're a Squallite, why do you have blue eyes? I thought they all had orange eyes."

Michael put down his fork and stared. "I wear contacts. It's also why I let my hair cover the tips of my ears. I might be a

Squallite, but I don't like to be discriminated against because of my race, so I try to look a little human. So people think twice."

Her face flushed, and she went back to playing with her food. "Oh, I'm sorry. I didn't realize. I didn't mean to upset you."

Michael pushed his hair back to reveal his pointless ears. "Don't sweat it, you didn't know. It's not something I brag about but will tell if I am asked."

Skyler stared into Michael's unnatural blue eyes. "Huh. I thought they were just alien, but with a closer look I can see how fake they are." Skyler leaned across the table and stared into Michael's eyes. "So you wear contacts, but you don't have a vision problem?"

"I do see electricity sometimes, usually when there is a break or something in a wire, but my vision is perfect. The optometrist told me I have the best eyes he has seen in a long time. These are glare-resistant colored contacts, nothing special. So when I look at a light I don't see the warm fuzziness, which helps with these dumb humming florescent light bulbs. It's the twenty-third century. You think they would have discontinued the stupid fluorescent light bulbs by now."

"I thought they used the bulbs because they are the cheapest?" Skyler commented.

Michael scoffed. "They are not the cheapest, especially with today's technology. If they were smart, they would have a solar laser go into the hollow-tube where the lights we have now had been, and the light would reflect. Then they would put a protective glass over the tubes and it would light them from one power source, all at once all day long, and take little power. And if it's still daylight when we turn the lights off, we can store energy for later. But the school says it's unreliable and would cost too much to convert."

"You think things would be more advanced in the twenty-third century."

Skyler added. "Like sex."

"What the fuck!" Kax's jaw dropped.

Skyler kept a straight face. "Ya, you would think with how long people have been having sex they would have found better toys and lube, but no, you're stuck with condoms. Those give you a three-minute orgasm feeling but without having one that long and toys that can..."

Kax put up her hand. "We got the message. Please don't tell us more details about your sex life."

Finally, I got Kax's attention. Skyler grinned. "I don't have to tell you, but I can show you."

She shifted uncomfortably. "I'm not sure whether I am more grossed out or disturbed, but I don't want to know what you do in bed."

Michael cut in before Skyler could say anything else. "So Kax, I noticed you have cat-like ears. Can you tell me what your species is?"

She tossed her hair. "Catillion. We're what you would call cat-like people. Some of the children have tails, but you don't see that too often anymore."

"So, you're a Catillion. I have heard of them. Your race is new to Earth. Isn't that like last generation or two?" Michael said.

She smiled with pride. "Yes. On Dad's side, I'm the first born on Earth and then on my mother's side, I'm a second gen. What about you?"

"I'm a Squallite. I know they were one of the first to make an alliance with Earth, but I am a first generation. My father immigrated to Earth and then had me." His gaze pointed to Skyler. "What's your history?"

Skyler picked his head up from his plate. "Well, I was born in space on one of my dad's missions and was raised on Earth and have a long lineage that can date back to… Um, I don't like to brag."

Michael scoffed. "Now that's a first."

Kax gave Michael a high five.

They were about finished their lunch when an Asian girl came up to fetch Kax. Before she left, Skyler drew a piece of paper out of his pocket and handed it to Kax. "Here's my room number. Stop by whenever you have time."

Kax hesitantly took the paper and waved goodbye.

Skyler changed focus over to Michael, with stars in his eyes. "Do you think she will ever fall for me?"

Michael shook his head. "Not if you keep up your attitude, you need to lay off the chicks and act mature. She's a sweet girl, she likes class."

A devilish smile crossed Skyler's face. "Class, you say. I can do that."

Michael picked up his and Skyler's empty trays and stood. "Come on. We should be getting ready for class, too."

"She is an amazing woman, isn't she?" With his head in the clouds, he followed Michael down the hall.

***

Skyler sat in the class not paying attention. He tuned out the instructor as he mentally replayed how cute Kax looked in her short skirt and leggings. Her royal purple uniform brought out her eyes. He slowly drifted off into a fantasy of passion, imagining her light tan soft skin, her shining gold cat-like eyes, her mid-length strawberry blonde hair and the curls flowing down her back. Her large breasts and a curvaceous figure were the finishing touches, which made her the perfect woman in his fantasy. Keeping the image in his mind, he slowly drifted off to sleep.

BOOM! A loud crash resonated throughout the school. Skyler jumped up and rushed towards the window with the rest of the class. Outside, a foreign silver almond-like spacecraft was shooting randomly at the school. His head thundered. Damn, another attack. There must be a war on its way.

He left class and ran through the halls. Got to come up with a plan. Where am I even going?

He was determined to save the school he loved.

By chance, he spotted Kax in the hall. "Kax!" he called out.

She didn't hear him.

He ran towards her, reached out and grabbed her arm before she returned to class.

She instinctively pushed him away. "What the heck do you think you're doing? And what is going on? I was in the bathroom when the alarm went off."

Skyler stopped his huffing and puffing, trying to catch his breath. "Sorry, I tried to call to you. There is another attack, and this time, there are at least two fighters shooting at the school. We need to stop it. Kax, you're a pilot. If we got a small fighter, could you help me?"

Kax gaped at him. "You want to go out there and fight back? We're inexperienced. We don't have the strength."

Skyler panted. "Listen, I know that, but we have to do something."

She gathered her thoughts. "They have officers who will be taking care of this. We need to stay safe."

Skyler took a minute to plan. He knew that was true, they would be sending all officers and fourth year and higher cadets to go and fight these things. But that wasn't going to hold him back. "They can always use more help. Come on."

They ran down the hall together until she suddenly stopped short.

"Skyler, we shouldn't be doing this. They have officers for these kinds of things."

Skyler smirked. "Trust me, I know what we're doing. And you may call me Captain."

She rolled her eyes. "Fine, I will do it, but if we get in trouble, it is your fault." She and Skyler raced as fast as they could. There were lives at stake.

They got to the hangar, filled with other more experienced cadets and officers. Skyler stood in the back, trying to stay hidden in all the chaos. He rushed to the gray screen. "Kax, could I please have your cadet code to access your fighter?"

She moved him aside. "I'll do it. We're not supposed to give these out." She used her security code to get them her training fighter. It was assigned to her for class use only. Then she scanned her key card for access to the fighter and turned to Skyler. "We damage this in any way and I will kill you."

They climbed in the fighter and prepared to take off. There was so much chaos going on, it was likely that no one noticed them fly out of there. Skyler checked the radar. He saw three enemy fighters near him, all similar to the one that attacked the first day of school. He told Kax to veer right to get to the side of them and then turn to the left and fire. Boom, a hit!

It brushed the side, but it was a hit. The fighter turned a little, getting ready to aim at Skyler. "Shoot now! As many as possible!"

They noted that the fighter was getting into the target range. Kax fired the guns as many times as possible, hoping to hit or disable the ship before it could fire back on them. Boom! A direct hit on the enemy fighter.

Skyler looked around as it crashed into the track field. It would be best to continue this fight outside of the school grounds.

"Kax, get the enemy's attention and fly this fighter as high as it can go. Make sure we are not near the school or the surrounding city."

Kax kept her eyes on the target. "Aye, Captain."

She flew right past the fighters, distracting them, and soon others followed on their trail. Kax was doing her best and noticed the green light blinking on her control panel. "Captain, we're getting an incoming message. Do you want to me answer it?"

If I answer that I could be ordered to stop, and both me and Kax will be in real trouble, or I can ignore it and say there is something wrong with the machine…

But he knew the only way to be a great captain was to answer and face his fate head on. He leaned over and clicked the button. "This is Cadet Therris speaking. How may I assist you?"

A booming feminine voice blared from the intercom. "Cadets, this is Fleet Admiral Davis, and I demand you and Cadet Tillion return to the academy immediately, or face severe disciplinary action!"

Skyler shook his head. "I'm sorry, Fleet Admiral, but I can't do that. We're in the middle of an attack, and I know that the forces need all the help they can get. That's all I am trying to do."

Skyler saw another fighter coming for them. "Kax, fire at three o'clock!"

Boom! Direct hit.

Skyler went back to the intercom. "Sorry, that was another one. Two down. How's that for a cadet, Fleet Admiral Davis?"

"You will get yourself killed. Get down here now or face expulsion!" Fleet Admiral Davis shouted.

Skyler peered into Kax's wide eyes and gave her a cheerful smile. "I'd rather lose two lives than a thousand, because if I'm not helping, there will be more deaths. If you don't like it, talk to Fleet Admiral Cane. Thank you for your concern, but I have a base to save." He hit the off switch and cut the communication.

Kax let out a sigh of relief.

Skyler glanced back at Kax and regained his confidence. New fighters kept showing up. She kept firing. She tried her best and blasted as many as they could. There were not many left to fight now. All the enemy fighters seemed to be gone, and most of the allied fighters were returning to dock. Kax turned the fighter back. Skyler exhaled a deep remorseful breath. "If you get into any trouble, I'm sorry. I don't know what to expect down there."

Kax put on a brave face as she landed the fighter in the hangar. "Whatever happens, it was worth being a hero and saving the lives that we did."

Once parked, she stood up and gave Skyler a hug. "I will stand behind you, Captain."

He hugged her tight, not wanting to let go. He took another deep breath, hit the door opener and stepped out. Outside the fighter, Fleet Admiral Cane awaited them with a box in his hand. "Cadet Therris and Cadet Tillion, due to your bravery and courage I would like to give you these."

He handed them the boxes; they both contained medals. Their eyes popped in shock. "And I must also give you these."

The cadets read over the letter he had handed them. "We're suspended?" Skyler asked. "For two weeks? How does that work when you live here?"

Kax hit Skyler in the arm. "Don't ask questions, it could have been a lot worse."

Fleet Admiral Cane chuckled at their reactions. "That is right, Cadet Tillion, and if it weren't for me, it would be worse. That is why I am giving you your medals here and not in a ceremony. We don't want to shine a light on cadets breaking rules and getting rewards. But two weeks is the minimum punishment I can give you as well as a very stern warning. If you do it again, I will have to give you a real punishment. As for where you can stay, if you have a place off campus, like your mother's house, then you can stay there, but if you don't, I will have to find you a job to do in exchange for staying here. Any problems?"

Skyler lowered his head. It was obvious Cane was talking indirectly to Skyler.

Kax maintained a stern face. "There will be no problem, sir. I have a place to stay. Thank you for being so kind."

The fleet admiral's gaze fell on Skyler. "You do have a place to stay, don't you?"

Skyler didn't want to talk about the life he left behind. "It's complicated, sir. I can't say for sure right now."

The fleet admiral took a deep breath. "If you have any problems, please see me in my office in the morning."

They both understood. "Yes, sir!"

They walked the hall together. "Hey, Kax. Why don't you come and see my room? Not as a pickup. I mean, really hang out. We have the rest of the day off now."

Her mouth curved. "You know after today, that sounds like a nice idea."

Skyler smiled in contentment.

They traveled back to the room. Skyler hopped onto his bed, sitting with legs folded. "So what do you think of the room?"

Kax admired the sky-blue walls and basic design. "Not too bad. Reminds me of my room, but the girls' dorm is pink."

He smirked, picturing it in his mind. "Of course it is. So the other bed is Michael's, and we share the closet and desk. That's it."

"Hey, what's with the boxes? Skyler, do you have a place to stay during the two weeks?"

Skyler averted his gaze, trying to avoid the question. "Well, like he said, I can stay here and work."

Michael entered the room and instantly spotted Kax standing in the center of the room. "Kax, I saw a 652 flying. Let me guess, you two didn't listen to the rules?"

Kax turned her head away and smiled. "That could have been any 652, they assign them to most of the pilot cadets."

Michael gave Skyler a shifty gaze. "You love to brag, so was it you two who shot down the fighter that landed on the track?"

Skyler tried to hold the truth back to bug Michael, but it didn't work. "Ya, it was us. I was running to the hangar. I bumped into Kax, and we went and took the fighter. Oh, and we got medals!" Skyler yanked the small dark wood box out of his pocket, and opened it to show Michael. "See, isn't it shiny? We can't brag, but I have two medals in three months. I'm on a roll. They will have to promote me soon."

Michael let Skyler ramble as he examined the medal. He focused his attention to Kax. "So what else happened?"

She rubbed her arms. She was trembling. With hesitation, she answered. "We're also suspended for two weeks, so Skyler and I are going there to hang out at my dad's cabin. It's about an hour off campus."

Skyler's brow shot up. All eyes were on Kax. Michael peered back at Skyler and back at Kax. "So are you two going to use it as a private getaway?"

Kax's face became beet red. "No, not like that. My dad has been bugging me to help clean up the cabin, and it isn't far from here. It's a lot closer than my dad's house. I was going to go up on the weekend, but now with the extra time, I might as well stay. It's a three-bedroom cabin, so there's plenty of room for Skyler to stay. It's a great place, up in the mountains south of here. You could come, too, if you like, but you have school."

Michael considered the offer. "You know, if it is only an hour away, I don't see why I can't go back and forth to school each day. It would be nice to get out of this stuffy room."

Kax clapped. "That sounds great. I'll give my dad a call. He can give us a ride."

Skyler got up and went over to Kax and whispered. "He's only coming because he'll miss me."

Michael leaned in. "More like I have wheels."


Chapter 5

Kax was packing in her dorm room when the door opened behind her. Her roommate backed into the room, kissing a strange guy. Kax crossed her arms. "Ona, what did I tell you? No guys here."

Ona kissed the guy one more time. "See you later, sexy."

The guy patted Ona on the butt. "I'll see you later." He left the room.

Kax shot a glare at her roommate. "Why did you bring him here?"

"We weren't going to have sex. We already did that, he was just bringing me back to the room." Ona sat on the bed. "Are you going somewhere?"

Kax sat on her bed and faced her roommate. "I have been suspended for two weeks."

"Goody two shoes Kitty Kax? What did you do?"

"Don't call me Kitty Kax. I hate that nickname. I'm not a cat!" She sighed. "It's that guy Skyler's fault."

Her roommate leaned in closer. "Oh, tell me more. Did you two get caught having sex in your shuttle?"

"No!" Kax snapped. "I'm not like you. I don't sleep with random men!"

"Skyler Therris, right? He's the cute blond I saw you having lunch with, right? He's not random or a stranger. I would sleep with him."

Kax's face went red. "Ew, it's Skyler. Don't say things like that!"

Her roommate got up and started changing out of her uniform. "Why, do you like him?"

Kax flopped on the bed and buried her face in her pillow. "I don't know. He is very handsome, but I don't know if I'm willing to trust him."

Ona finished buttoning her pink and green flannel pajamas. "Trust him? What are you talking about?"

Kax sat back up. "I don't like talking about this but when I was in high school, I dated a guy like Skyler. He was the hottest guy in school and all the women wanted him. I agreed to go out with him because he seemed nice and told me he cared. I didn't want to have sex. I wanted to wait, but he pressured me into it. He used me. He had sex with me for two months then found someone else and dumped me. He made me try things I didn't want to do, but I agreed to because I was young, naïve and was convinced no one else wanted me. After he threw me away, the next two guys after were not much better. I don't want that to happen again."

Ona joined Kax on the bed. "I'm sorry. I had no idea. So you think Skyler is like this guy?"

"I am not sure. They both have the same 'I'm sexy and can get anyone I want' attitude."

"I haven't slept with Skyler, but what the other girls say, he is a kind and caring guy who just has a high sex drive. He does seem to go for the bad girls, but you're a good girl. Maybe he is interested in more than just sex?"

Kax rolled her eyes. "He will probably stay with me until he gets me pregnant and then run off."

Ona laughed. "Aren't you on some sort of birth control?"

Kax shook her head. "Haven't had sex since my prom. I don't see a need to be on it."

"I've heard Skyler always uses a condom so you would be safe. I'm sure he is not a bad guy. You should give him a chance."

Kax sighed. "I'll consider your words, but I don't know if I am willing to trust any guy right now."

"What about the tall dark haired one? You interested in him?"

"Michael?" Kax blushed. "He's handsome, but I don't think I'm his type. He is more of a big brother."

"Good, because there's a rumor going around that he's gay."

Kax stood up and resumed her packing. "I don't think Michael is gay. I think he is just shy."

Ona went back over to her own bed. "You know, if Skyler was bi, you could have both."

Kax shuddered and covered her ears. "I'm not listening anymore. You go to bed. I've got to finish packing."

Ona climbed into her bed. "Give Skyler a chance before someone else steals him away, that's all I am saying."


Chapter 6


Morning came sooner than they expected. Michael might have told them that he was going to go to class during the two weeks, but he needed the break from school. Once he got to the top of his class, he didn't see much point in staying. The worst part was that no one would notice if he wasn't in class or not.

He went to the engineering building early to see if the instructor was there. The whole engineering building was a long narrow maze. It was for Squallites to stay in shape and flex their muscles when they needed to venture into small spaces. He made his way to the commodore's office on the other side of the maze. Then he knocked on the door. A deep voice came from within. "Come in."

Michael opened the door and entered the room. "Commodore Yantic, I need to talk to you."

Yantic raised his head from the papers on his desk. "Well then, have a seat Cadet Jones, and tell me what seems to be the problem?"

Michael sat down. "Sir, you know I am working hard and my grades are at the top of the class. But I was wondering if I could take some time off?"

Yantic narrowed his eyes at Michael. "Why would you want to take time off? And how much time?"

"Two weeks', sir. Reason, sir, is I don't want to be an engineer."

Yantic let out a long sigh. "If you don't want to be an engineer, then you might as well quit the forces now. You know that's not going to change anytime soon. But I sense there is something else the matter?"

Michael stared at his feet. "Sir, what is the point of me doing well in class? You know I have always been a good student and always worked hard. But what's the point? All of us Squallites have it drilled into our brains how to fix a wire. It's been passed down through generation to generation, and now we're all perfect at it. The class average is 97 percent. I don't see the point in studying anymore and continuing my work. I am only in the forces for the job security. It's not fair. I want to do more with my life."

Yantic nodded. "You're right, Michael, and we all want to do more. But until things change, this is the only option. Has your dad ever told you about what he went through before he joined the forces?"

"A little bit, sir. I know he bounced around from job to job making pennies, worried about being arrested if he made a mistake. That's why he convinced me to join the forces when I was old enough." Michael twiddled his thumbs.

"He was right to join. I know you want to be a captain and having a command cadet as a roommate is just feeding these delusions. But you're not wrong. I will give you the two weeks off. But I want you to clear your head. Things aren't going to change anytime soon. Be happy you have this opportunity."

"Thank you, sir."

When Michael returned to the dorm, Skyler and Kax were waiting in the room with their bags packed. Michael sighed at the fact he was leaving behind his room for a bit. He would miss it; he was starting to get used to this place.

Once they were ready, they made their way down to the academy's parking garage.

There was an antique 1980s motorcycle in the garage. Michael walked over to it and put his hand on the handlebars. "This is it."

"Nice ride!" Skyler exclaimed. "Whose is it and how did you get it?"

Michael mounted the bike. "It's mine. Dad got it for me a few years ago. Would you believe it, someone threw it out. There were a few parts missing, and it needed to be completely upgraded, but we engineers know how to do all that. But it's road safe as it passed inspection. The sidecar is the only thing I had to pay for. I bought it separate from a collector."

Kax took one of the helmets Michael handed her from his bag. He pulled out his keys.

"Sorry, but I only have two helmets," he told Skyler. "Is it okay if you ride without one or should I come back for you?"

Skyler checked out the bike. "Only if you let me take it for a spin?"

Michael chuckled. "Not now. Maybe later when we get there I might let you take it out. So do you want me to come back for you or not?"

Skyler fingered parts of the bike. "Naw, I'll ride without the helmet, I like to live on the edge."

Kax got into the sidecar and said, "I don't want you to get anymore brain damage. You'd better take mine." She went to remove her helmet.

Michael put his hand on her head and pushed on the helmet. "Skyler said he doesn't want a helmet. Let him make his own mistakes."

***

Michael pulled into the driveway of a fancy secluded log cabin in the mountains. The bike grumbled to a stop.

Skyler's jaw dropped. The house had modern solar panels and an electronic front door. He loved the large stone base on the first level and the wood siding. The large two-story cabin was gorgeous. Blown away, Skyler turned to Kax. "Wow, this place is amazing."

Kax scrambled off the bike. "The bike might be Michael's, but the cabin is mine."

She hurried up to the steps of the porch up to the front door. She fished a set of keys out of her pocket and unlocked the door. "This is my parents' cabin. Mom and Dad used to come up here a lot until my mom passed away. Now it's empty most of the time. That's why I get to use it."

They all stepped inside. The beauty of the polished hard wood, tall ceiling and fireplace in the living room astonished Skyler.

The inside had hardwood flooring and an enormous area rug, with a bearskin in front of a giant fireplace in the center.

"Wow, I don't think I have seen a place this nice in a long time," Michael said.

Kax blushed. "It is lovely, and very expensive to keep up. My dad wants to get rid of it because we don't use it that much."

The joy fell from Skyler's face. "He can't sell it. This is an amazing place, and it's too pretty to give up."

Kax giggled. "I keep telling my dad that but money talks. At least I can go here after school or on holidays for now as long as I have a ride."

"That is so handy," Michael said. "It's a great place. I wish my dad's place was this close."

Skyler headed into the kitchen through the hallway in the living room. When he saw the windows on the back wall of the kitchen, he ran to them and admired the view. "Hey, Michael, come see this. There's an outdoor stone barbecue, and it overlooks the lake!"

Michael rushed over to Skyler's side at the full-length windows. "This is an impressive place. How did you guys ever score a place like this?"

Kax went over to the boys. "I don't know who built this place, but my mom was promoted to admiral after this was built. She wasn't an admiral long. She died when I was eight."

Skyler took a break from watching the view and went and gave Kax a hug. "Don't get upset. I know what it's like, my dad died when I was five."

Kax tensed up from the surprise hug. "I wasn't upset. I was telling a story. I got over my mom's death a long time ago."

Skyler stopped hugging Kax. "I wanted to have an excuse to hug you is all."

Michael laughed.

Kax shook her head. "Come on, let me show you the rest of the house."

They went to the large kitchen where there was a huge fridge, an ice maker, and stone top counters. It was old-fashioned style, which meant that there was no food replicator. There was a kitchen island made of solid maple, with three seats and a small kitchen table with five seats. The door led them to an outdoor patio with a table and chairs.

Skyler loved every inch of the place. He was at peace here, in this atmosphere. He went right to the fridge. Michael admired the house. "This place is amazing! Who knew they even built homes this close to the academy!"

Kax stood next to a chair at the kitchen island. "There aren't many, but there are a few. All cabins for the lake, but we all have to go to the city for food. It's really not that far out. There is a tiny convenience store, but it only sells camping food and supplies. Really, if you're coming out here for a short time, you don't need tons of food. I thought I was going to give you guys a tour."

Skyler popped his head out of the fridge and rooted inside the top freezer. "Tour can be later. I think I will live in the kitchen once we get food. All I've found is a box of fish sticks."

Kax looked embarrassed. "Oh, I guess it's been a while since my dad has been here. Well, Michael, want to give me a ride to the store?"

Michael eyed the silver-framed analog clock on the wall above the stove. "Sure, no problem. Do you want to go to the convenience store or one in the city?"

Skyler grabbed his stomach. "I skipped breakfast. Go to the small one. We don't need much. Get more fish sticks. I'll start with these."

He preheated the silver steel oven and found an old black baking sheet in the drawer under the oven. He worked on making the fish sticks.

Kax glanced at Michael. "Sounds good. We can go to the city tomorrow."

Michael walked back to the front door. Kax warned Skyler, "Don't burn the house down when we're gone. We shouldn't be too long. Is there anything besides fish sticks you want?"

Skyler thought about it. "How about some chips and hamburgers? More fish and beer are all I can think of right now."

"Sounds good to me. They should have that stuff there." She was about to leave the room when Skyler pulled a $100 bill out of his pocket. "This is for groceries."

Kax froze, and then took the money. "Thanks, Skyler, I'll use it well."

Skyler smiled and went back to the fish sticks. "Have a good time now."

\*\*\*

Kax glanced over her shoulder at Skyler as she moved towards the door.

Michael and Kax arrived at the camping store. It had old-fashioned gray wood panel walls and camping gear all over the walls and shelves. He scanned the aisles and noticed a cooler in the back.

Kax headed for the dry goods.

Michael fetched two boxes of fish sticks and went to find Kax. "Hey, I didn't ask you earlier, but what is the budget here? I don't want to overspend."

Kax lifted out her brown leather wallet. "Don't worry about the money, I've got it covered."

Michael walked back to the coolers. This time he grabbed a basket.

Kax grabbed a lot of snack food and some marshmallows along with a loaf of bread.

Michael found a few bottles of juice and a twelve pack for Skyler. They brought their baskets up to the front and unloaded them on the counter.

The man at the counter greeted them with a smile, "Good day, Kax. Long time no see. How are you doing?"

Kax smiled. "I'm doing good. I'm on holiday from the academy and came here to get some food."

He smiled and scanned the food and placed the items in a netted bag. "It's nice to see you, but does your dad know you are up here alone with a Squallite?"

Kax's jaw dropped. "Mr. Perkins, Michael is my friend and there is nothing wrong with him. He is a good friend of mine. My father is happy with my choice of friends."

Michael got an uneasy feeling.

"I'm sorry about that, Kax. I didn't mean to offend." Mr. Perkins leaned in closer to her. "But between you and me, I wouldn't trust him and his kind. They are not very trustworthy." Kax frowned, quickly paid the bill and got the hell out of there.

Michael helped Kax with the bags. He placed the groceries in the sidecar. He was about to get on the bike when Kax started to cry. He went over to Kax and circled his arm around her. "Hey, what's the matter?"

She turned and hugged Michael. "I'm sorry about that in there, who knew he would say anything like that? I never knew he felt like that."

Michael hugged Kax tight and smiled. "Hey, that's not your job to worry about. These things, they're mine, I'm used to it. Yes, he was rude, but what can you do?"

"You're a nice person. That's what you are, a person, not anything else."

He wiped the tears off her face. "You can't change them all, but you can pick your battles."

She hugged a little tighter before letting go. "I guess you're right. I know people don't care for my race, but why do they care so much about yours?"

"I guess because were hard workers and have more talents than humans. If they can't use us, they hate us. But it's not your fight. It's the cross I was born to bear, but one day the world will change. That's where I have hope."

Kax's tears dried, and a smile crossed her face. "I'm glad you have hope."

Michael smiled too and brushed her hair back. "Come on, let's get going before Skyler eats the furniture."


\*\*\*

Back at the house, Skyler found a music player and blasted his playlist. He was dancing to one of his favorite songs when they got back.

Kax opened the door and saw Skyler dancing. She stopped Michael from coming in. She pressed her finger over her mouth. They both got a kick out of watching him for a bit before Skyler moved closer to the door and noticed the two of them watching him.

Skyler froze. "Um, hi."

Kax and Michael entered, laughing. Michael was carrying the bags of food. "So I'm guessing you had a fun time while we were gone."

Skyler was still frozen and unsure of what to say.

Kax picked up one of the boxes of fish sticks from Michael's bag and handed them to Skyler. "Here's the fish sticks you asked for."

Skyler laughed and headed to the kitchen with the rest of them.

Kax turned the oven back on. "I see you ate the whole box of old fish sticks. Now Michael and I have to make food."

Skyler headed over to Michael. "So did you get the beer?"

Michael sighed. "Help me put the groceries away and then you can have some."

"Fair enough." Skyler picked up a bag and placed it on the island. He started unpacking. They finished putting away the food without incident.

Kax worked with the food that they bought. She made some hot dogs for them and brought them the plate. "I'm sorry that we don't have better food but hey, at least its food."

The guys dug in. Michael spoke to Kax. "No problem, it's food, and it's not the freezer burnt fish sticks Skyler ate."

Skyler looked embarrassed, but brushed it off. "Ya, well like you said, food is food."

He opened a can of beer and chugged it.

Chapter 7

Evening came and Skyler had been enjoying the view of the lake. Michael was working on his schoolwork on his tablet. Kax was checking the rooms to make sure they were in top condition. She entered the kitchen. "Hey, guys, let me show you where you are sleeping for the next few days."

Skyler stepped in and Michael put his tablet away. They both followed Kax up the hardwood staircase, where she pointed out the guest rooms and a bathroom they could share.

Then she led them to the master bedroom. She opened the door. "This is my bedroom. It has the attached bathroom so you guys won't have to deal with me."

It had a huge double bed, dresser, vanity desk and a large bay window. Skyler sprinted into the room and hopped on the bed. "I think you mean our room."

He winked at Kax and lay down.

Kax rolled her eyes standing at the doorway with Michael. "No, Skyler, you have your own room. Please get off my bed."

Skyler grinned and got off the bed. "Ok, but if you want me you know where to find me."

Kax laughed. "Don't hold your breath."

The next and final part of the tour was at the end of the hall. Kax opened the last door. "This is your room, Skyler. I hope you like it."

Skyler examined the room. There was a large window with long curtains and the double bed had a nice light green bedding and a dresser. It was a very classy log cabin room. Skyler smiled and turned to Kax. "This room is wonderful. Thank you for everything."

"It was the least I could do." She gently smiled back.

Michael checked his watch. "Thanks for the tour of the rooms, but do we have to go to bed now or can we stay up for a bit more?"

Kax laughed. "Oh, you don't have to go to bed. I was just showing you all the rooms. Come on, we can go downstairs. I have lots of games and we can play some, and then have supper. It will be fun."

The gang headed downstairs and pulled out a copy of Monopoly hologram edition. They played well into the night.

Chapter 8

Skyler stretched as he sat up in his bed. He glanced over at the clock and saw the clock flash 7 a.m. How did that happen? I woke up before the alarm?

He peeked out the window seeing the sunrise. Sunrise. I haven't seen a sunrise in how long. Now what am I going to do, no one else is up. He got out of bed, got dressed and trekked downstairs. He grabbed a beer and headed out to the deck to enjoy the view of the half-frozen lake. He watched the sunrise and sniffed the cold forest air.

Not long after, Michael came over and leaned on the railing next to Skyler. "So you sleep well?"

Skyler let out a big relaxed breath. "Ya, I love it here. I don't think I have felt so relaxed in my entire life, this is truly a wondrous place."

Michael patted his hand on Skyler's back. "I know exactly how you feel."

Skyler turned his head to his friend. "There is something magical about this place, like I was meant to be here or something."

Michael shot another glance at the view. "I don't feel that strongly, but I am glad you are happy about being here. I am curious, why did Kax invite you up here?"

"Not sure why she did, but I know she was trying to help." He took a sip of his beer. "See, the fleet admiral told us we couldn't be in the rooms for two weeks and he asked us if we had a place to go and, well, I could find a place, but when I moved to the academy I made it my home."

"I get it now. I still live with my dad when I'm not in school because he's a commodore. He is not home much and I'm home in the summer, so it's more like we are roommates. It's only logical."

"That would be nice." Skyler pictured him and his dad doing the same thing. "Damn, I miss my dad now. You jerk."

Michael narrowed his brow. "Dude, I'm sorry, that was totally not my plan. You going to be okay?"

Skyler finished his beer and let out a long sigh. "I'm not going to cry, but ya, I like thinking of my dad. But the academy reminds me too much of him. It's been bothering me a lot lately, that's all."

Michael put his arm around Skyler, giving him a close hug. "You said he used to be a captain. What ship? And how did he die?"

Skyler turned his frown into a smile of pride. "My father was the captain of the HMSS Blackstar, and he died in the line of duty. There was a surprise attack from some aliens. He saved his entire crew, but he went down with the ship. I was five when he died and I miss him like crazy."

"Now that is sad, I didn't realize it was like that. What did your mom do?"

The light in Skyler's eyes faded and he mumbled, "She did her own thing I guess. She did get remarried, but he is not in the forces. He has some government job and is a total asshole."

Michael dropped the subject. "So have you ever seen your dad's ship?"

Skyler brushed his hair back. "I saw it when I was a kid when my dad was alive, but since he died, I heard the ship was destroyed, it burnt up and that it's all gone."

"Well, then. When we get back to the academy, I must show it to you. The HMSS Blackstar was one of the first ships to do five jumps on half the fuel. It was one of the best ships ever made. Even though all that is left mostly looks like a pile of junk metal, the forces are still holding on to it. When we get back, I will show you the ship. It's in a place only the engineers are allowed to go."

Skyler beamed. "It's still around? Wow! It would be great to see it again. I wish it were still in commission. I would love to be the Capitan of the Blackstar and start a legacy with the ship. But I know that's not how things work."

Michael laughed. "That is so true, but even if it was in commission it's thirteen years out of date. No way it is going to be useful; it only does five jumps. Most ships do nine to eleven jumps now. It was an experimental engine that worked, so you can't upgrade it. I even heard they are working on a twelve jump machine but that won't be out until about… after we graduate."

Skyler lip twitched. "Thank you, for knocking down my dreams, I'll remember that for later."

Kax had overheard most of their conversation and was shocked about their family pasts. Not wanting the boys to know she overheard them, she went right into the kitchen and started making them all breakfast. After a few minutes of cooking, the aroma of the food got the guys to come in.

Michael sniffed the air. "Mmm, smells good. What are you cooking?"

Kax checked over her shoulder and saw them sitting down at the table. She flipped over the food in the frying pan. "Fish, but not fish sticks. This is the package of frozen fish Michael got for us yesterday."

Skyler looked over at Michael. "Nice, you like fish too."

Michael snorted. "I don't mind it, but we're in a cabin, it's like camping. Fish seemed the better choice. Its real fish, too. Not the fake stuff you like."

Kax giggled, bringing a plate of food over to the table. "Well, if it means anything, I like fish too."

Skyler made the hand gesture on his head to represent cat ears. "Ya, no question about that."

Kax took Skyler's plate back and put it on the island. "You want your food, go and get it. I'm not serving you again."

Skyler put on his puppy dog eyes. "Oh, come on. You have been in such a bad mood since I beat you last night at Monopoly."

Michael scoffed before taking a bite of his food. "You haven't won. We didn't finish the game and I think, according to the computer, that I am a tad in the lead."

Her face smug, she bit into her food. "He's right, so no gloating until it's over."

Skyler shut up, got up and grabbed his plate.

Michael turned his attention to Kax. "I know we don't have enough food to last us all the two weeks so do you want me and Skyler to give you a break and go out shopping later?"

Kax paused. "That seems like a good idea, I wouldn't mind the time alone."

Michael peered over at Skyler. "It's decided. We are going to go grocery shopping later in the city."

Skyler finished his plate of food. "Sounds good to me."


Chapter 9


Michael took Skyler with him to the city, giving Kax some time alone to relax and clean up. Once in the grocery store, Skyler was having fun bugging Michael in the store.

Michael was regretting taking Skyler with him. He was also trying to avoid another one of Skyler's 'Marshmallow fights.' They trudged up and down the aisles and Skyler found something to throw in the air for a solo game of catch. Michael was missing Kax more and more. He collected the food that they needed like: meat, veggies, and fruit. While he watched Skyler gathering unnecessary items like candy, and chips, he remarked, "I hope if we ever have to pack for a survival mission, you're not in charge of the food."

Skyler smirked, plucking a box of cookies off the shelf, "You are no fun. You know that, right? Look at the cart, you are getting the survival food, and I'm getting the snacks. You can never have enough snacks."

Michael reached into his pocket and brought out his wallet. "How about I give you some money and you buy what you want at the liquor store?"

Skyler lifted out his own fat wallet. "I should be the one giving you money for the food. I have it all covered."

He opened his wallet and handed Michael $300. There was clearly more in there. "I don't think this stuff will come to that much but it's good to have extra. I'll see you later. The liquor store is next door." He waved and headed off.

Michael was dumbstruck by how much money Skyler had in his wallet. Who walks around with that much money?

\*\*\*

At the liquor store, Skyler ambled up and down the aisles enjoying browsing at all his favorites. His smile widened at the sight of the shining colored glass bottles. He loaded up the cart. How much do I plan to drink? I can't take this back to the academy…

He put a bottle or two back and took a moment to think more logically. He got more of his absolute favorites and figured Kax would probably let him store the stuff at her place. He searched around the store and noticed an attractive girl with light blue skin picking out a bottle of wine. He sidled up to her. "You know, that is a good choice you've got there, I hope you are not drinking alone?"

Startled, she jerked around to see Skyler. "Oh, this is a gift for a friend. I really don't drink."

Skyler grinned, moving a bit closer to her and the shelf. "That is not the kind of wine you would give away, look at the price. You want something cheaper that goes with food, as to say, 'I thought of you but enjoy your meal.'"

The girl giggled. "What do you recommend?"

Skyler picked up a bottle of Hologram Dust. "This one. It's new, but it is a lot better than others. You're fine to give this one away."

She batted her eyelashes at him and accepted the bottle. "And, for myself, if I were to drink alone?"

He gazed into her bright blue eyes. "A beautiful woman like you should never drink alone."

He grabbed a bottle of Orion Sparkling Wine and handed it to her. "This is the kind you drink with someone you want to have a good time with."

She blushed, accepted the bottle from him and placed it in the basket with the other one. He whipped a piece of paper out of his pocket. "Here's my number. Call me."

He brushed his hand against her lower back and gently pulled her close, leaning almost to kiss her. He seduced her with his eyes and put on a charming smile. Her face was reddened by his charm.

He watched her put his number in her pocket. He knew she was definitely going to call him later.

Michael finished shopping for food. He wished he could have bought more, but there was not enough to fit in the sidecar. He noticed Skyler was carrying a few cases of alcohol. He let out a big sigh. "You do realize we're limited for space. Where are we going to fit all the food, let alone your beer?"

Skyler examined the sidecar. He was not thinking about the space inside the vehicle. "I don't know, but we can't leave this stuff here. How about we fill up the sidecar and I ride on your back?"

Michael exhaled, considering the size of the sidecar, trying to figure out how all of it would fit. "Okay, but if you let go, I'm not going back for you."

Skyler laughed and got on the bike after Michael once they had packed everything into the sidecar.

\*\*\*

Kax had just gotten off the holo-phone with her father when she heard the bike pull up. She waited by the window and watched the guys unload the supplies. She went to open the door.

As Skyler stepped inside carrying a case of beer, he winked at Kax. "There's my lovely lady. I missed you. Did you miss me?"

She rolled her eyes while holding the door. She had the urge to close it on Skyler. "Yes, I did, for some odd reason. I will never understand why."

Skyler playfully craned his neck in an attempt to kiss Kax. "I love you, too."

She lightly shoved Skyler way from her. "Don't try to kiss me."

"I'll win you over one day." He carried the case to the kitchen and placed it on the counter.

Kax ignored Skyler; it was one idea she hadn't tried with him.

Michael had slipped in past them with his portion of the groceries. He was unpacking the food and keeping out of the conversation.

Kax closed the door and headed over to the kitchen to help with the unpacking.

Skyler didn't help. He decided to check his tablet for messages instead. His eyes popped when he looked down at his tablet.

"Hey, you two. I would love to help, but I have someone I need to call. I'll be back later." He didn't wait for a response and carried the tablet upstairs with him.

Kax and Michael shared a glance. Kax was polite and called out, "Okay, do what you need to. You know where to find us."

Kax and Michael finished putting away the food.

Michael waited for Skyler to be out of sight. "You know he means no harm by the things he does."

"I know, but I'm not one to give into guys like him."

"Well, that's good. So are we going to get working on supper or do you want a snack for now?"

Kax's stomach growled. "You know, let's not make food yet because I can make pasta later and it will be quick. We can get the Monopoly game set back up and wait for Skyler. He shouldn't be too much longer."

Michael rubbed his rumbling tummy. "I am not that hungry either. Sounds good, if he does take a long time, we can play another game like truth or dare."

She didn't buy it. "You really want to play that game? Doesn't seem your style."

Michael laughed and shook his head. "I'm fine. I'll grab some snacks to hold me over to suppertime. It sounds like a fun game to play with you." He winked.

She scrunched her face, checking to see if Michael was okay.

His shoulders slouched. "I was trying to be like Skyler, it seems to work for him."

"Ya, don't do it again it is so not you." She tossed back her hair and smirked.

They both shared a laugh then made their way back to the living room and waited for Skyler.

It was almost an hour later when Skyler came back down. His eyes were narrow and his cheeks puffed. He didn't make eye contact with anyone.

Kax felt like saying something, but wasn't sure how to say it.

Skyler peered over and saw the game. "Don't finish the game without me. I'm going to win."

Michael scoffed. "No, we're playing your other favorite game. Shot glass chess."

Skyler face drooped. "Hey, no one is to touch the booze without me."

"No. We're not. We're playing Life, and we're about done, then we can finish Monopoly." Kax shifted in her seat towards Skyler. "Is there anything wrong? Who was that phone call to?"

"I will be fine. Just was a call from someone I haven't talked to in a while." He walked over to the fridge and removed a beer. He came back and sat at the table in the middle of them.

He is hiding something. I am going to have to get to the bottom of this. She shifted back towards Michael. "Come on, let's finish this game."

Skyler sipped his beer. "You know, I'm the winner of Monopoly."

"The game's not over yet. I could still beat both you boys."

Chapter 10

Morning came and Kax woke to the sound of Skyler running down the hall screaming, "Snow is here, snow is here!"

She and Michael stepped out of their rooms, rubbing their disgruntled faces. According to the clock, it was 7 a.m. She could tell Michael was not happy to have been woken up.

They trudged down to the kitchen where they saw Skyler rolling around in the snow in the backyard in his underwear.

"Since you're dressed and I am just wearing this robe, could you go and get the little idiot before he gets sick?" Kax asked.

"It would be my pleasure."

Michael darted out after Skyler and tried to catch him. "Listen, you might love snow, but you are going to get all wet and cold and maybe sick."

It seemed Skyler was having more fun running away from Michael than actually playing in the snow. He was not going to go back in without a fight.

Kax watched the two run around. She stroked the sides of her face. If I didn't hate getting wet, I would be out there myself.

Finally, after a few minutes Michael caught Skyler and dragged him in by his arm. Melted snow covered both of them as they dripped water all over the floor.

Kax rushed to the laundry room and grabbed two towels. While the boys were drying off, she made hot chocolate on the stove. After a few minutes, she poured them each a cup. "I used the marshmallows that were expired. They are solid as rocks, but the warm liquid will melt them and they will be fine."

Michael and Skyler took theirs to the couch. Kax fetched blankets from the hall closet and activated the gas fireplace. Michael regarded the fireplace oddly. "Why do you have a gas fireplace? I thought they stopped making them like sixty years ago."

"I have no idea, maybe that's how old this place is?"

Michael examined the fireplace. "Oh, you know what? This is probably not gas at all. It's this new thing called carbon fluids. They spray an invisible liquid on the logs. It only does it once, and it lasts for hours. The same five logs can last a week or something. That is very new, like twenty years old."

Kax sat in the chair next to the couch. "That would make more sense, because I am certain the gas fireplaces are banned. If not, I know they are hazardous."

Michael sat down on the couch and drank some of his hot chocolate. "Only thing about that is you can't convert the old fireplace to a carbon fireplace. But this place seems too expensive for it to have been built twenty years ago."

He pondered the origin of this cabin.

Skyler was drinking his cocoa. "Isn't it great we have lots of snow?"

"I guess it is." Kax crossed her legs and sipped her drink. "I know the city doesn't get snow, but we still do because there is slightly less pollution up here. It's usually not this much though."

Skyler stared into his drink. "I lived outside of the city and it always snowed there. But it was less and less each year. We used to get about two feet when I was a kid. I miss that. Now we're lucky if we get six inches."

"Then I should take you guys to see my family's home world, planet Squall. Their winters are bad. You are snowed in until the rain comes in the spring." Michael finished his drink.

"So your home world is an ice planet?" Skyler narrowed his eyes.

Michael placed his cup on the coffee table. "No, but it is full of storms. Use a dictionary and look up Squall. You will find it quite interesting. We get lots of blizzards in the winter time."

Skyler hummed while he drank his cocoa. "Hey, Kax. Thanks for the hot cocoa. It is one of the best cups I ever had. And thanks for adding the marshmallows, too."

She winked while taking a sip. "You can't have cocoa without marshmallows."

\*\*\*

Nightfall came sooner than expected. Skyler was enjoying the view out on the porch, watching for the moon to light up the midnight sky and shine off the freshly fallen snow. He loved the glow of the light hitting the snow. It made him feel so at peace.

Michael came out and brought Skyler a jacket. "Why are you not wearing a coat? You're going to freeze."

Skyler smiled. "There's a fire in my heart that keeps me warm all the time."

"Are you saying my cooking is bad, because I think you just described heartburn?" Michael joked.

"No, it's the fire of determination." He paused. "Or stubbornness. People have given me two names for it."

Michael laughed and patted Skyler on the back. "Come on, it's almost midnight. Let's go in and have a snack."

Skyler didn't want to go in; he wanted to stay outside in this wonderful below zero weather.

Michael went back in the house while Skyler lingered outside for a few more minutes. Finally Skyler joined his friends on the living room couch.

Kax turned on the television. They were going to watch a movie, but the channel last left on was the news, which reported other attacks around the world.

Michael's face soured.

Kax was worried. "How much longer before you think we will declare war?"

Michael's hand shook. "I don't know, but this is not good. It can't be much longer. See, Earth has to jump past the planet Squall to get to Cassiopeia. But the Squallites aren't going to war with them, and we don't want our portals used for war. The Cassiopeians have another route. Earth is trying to make more portals. But it's not easy. We keep running into problems. It takes three months to build one portal but there have been reports of sabotage so it is delaying all efforts. Hopefully, Earth can convince the other Squallites to use their portals to go to war."

"You do realize if the Squallites don't let us go to war, that will hold back on their civil rights," Skyler spits out.

Michael shuffled his feet with a sigh. "I know. And they will be reduced more than they are now. But it's not that simple, the Squallites are at peace with all, so they have to keep both their allies safe."

"Worst part is the Cassiopeians haven't tried to fight us in about fifteen years and they admitted that the last war was a mistake, so why now? Are they tired of fighting themselves?" Kax pointed out.

"Cassiopeians, that's what they look like, the ones who cut my hand?" Skyler asked.

"That was nothing. They are the worst. They believe in war and hate peace. I have no idea why they want to go to war with us this time. Last time it was over territory in space but we have been honoring that. My dad used to support them, thinking they were a kind people who had their strange ways we didn't understand. But that isn't it. The situation with them has gotten worse. Another reason my dad came to Earth was that he supported the humans, not the Squallites' beliefs on the Cassiopeians."

Skyler remembered the horrible fangs and their long pointed horns on their heads. It was something he had seen a few times in his dreams. He didn't want to remember or think of them, he wanted them all gone. But something was oddly familiar about them.

Kax sighed. "So if we go to war, our generation of cadets is going to be sent to the front lines right after graduation."

"Which is why they're probably going easy on you two, because you're good at what you do and they aren't going to give up an able bodied cadet. At least not for goofing off," Michael pointed out.

Skyler agreed and spoke up. "So do your best to stay in for all seven years, because they will take you to war when you graduate."

Michael shook his head. "It won't matter. At four years, they can send you to finish your three remaining years on duty. They give you shit pay and the lowest rank. Or they will just graduate you early. But if they need you, they will take you. That's the boat I will be in for next year once I finish my fourth year. I may not be in combat, but I will most likely be on one of the combat ships."

Kax rubbed her arms. "This sucks. We are peaceful traders and explorers. Our ships are not made for war. They are made for science!" A tear sprang to her eye.

Michael changed seats and gave Kax a side hug. "Science makes war. We might be peaceful, but others see our technology and want it. Also, every ship may not be made for war, but it can be easily modified. This war will happen. The only question is how soon."

Skyler paused for a bit and watched the news. He was trying to figure out something. "We have portals around the Modorlean home world. I bet if they changed their angles about five degrees you'd slightly bypass the Cassiopeians world and they would not see us coming."

Michael contemplated the idea. "That may work, but it will take a little longer and it is hard to change the portals."

Kax perked up. "That still could work, because the ships do have a speed of their own. We can go and move the rest of the way, even if it takes longer. We bypass them so they will see it as a surprise attack. It will buy us time to get the Squallites' permission. The Modorlean don't like the Cassiopeians. They don't really like us, but they do prefer humans to most other races."

While they talked and shared their thoughts, Skyler typed out an e-mail on his tablet. When he hit send, the tablet made a 'ping' sound.

"What was that?" Michael inquired.

Skyler lowered the tablet onto the coffee table. "Oh, I sent our ideas to Fleet Admiral Cane. Maybe he can use some of them."

Michael glared. "You have the fleet admiral's personal e-mail address?"

Skyler looked at everyone's funny expressions. "Well, ya, doesn't everyone?"

"No. You have got to tell me what your connection to him is?" Michael stared at Skyler. "Also, do you really think that the fleet admiral will listen and use our ideas?"

"He just gave me the e-mail, it's not a big deal." Skyler let out a deep breath. "I hope he will take our ideas. It would be nice, but if not, what can we do?"

Michael gave up. "It is going to be hard on Earth, having an interstellar war at this point, we don't have the money. But when you are dealing with outside forces, you can't simply ignore them."

"Yup, I agree. This could be the beginning of the end for all of us." Kax gave an involuntary shudder.

Michael turned his head towards the clock. "It's late, let's go to bed and not think of this. We can eat our snacks and stuff tomorrow because that's another day."

Kax was clearly upset and shaky. "Ok, that sounds good to me."

Her nerves were too shot to clean up the mess. So Skyler carried the bowls and remaining snacks to the kitchen.

Michael held Kax's arm and helped her up the stairs. "It's not in our control, but even the strongest of us don't always have courage." He escorted Kax to her room. "You will be fine, don't you worry, okay? The war is not going to happen."

Kax gave Michael a weary smile.

Skyler got a blanket from the hall closet and retreated to one of the lounge chairs outside. He laid down and watched the night sky. The cold didn't bother him; he enjoyed the cold compared to most things. He wrapped the blanket around himself and grasped his beer. He laid there fantasizing about the stars.

\*\*\*

Late into the night, Kax was having problems sleeping. She got out of bed and knocked on Skyler's door. He wasn't there, so she slowly opened Michael's door. "Michael, are you awake?" She crept in.

Michael opened his eyes and spotted her at the foot of the bed. He looked like he was only wearing his boxers. "Kax, what are you doing here?"

"I'm really scared about the war. Can I sleep with you for comfort?"

"I don't see the harm."

Kax, wearing her pink fluffy robe, snuggled in the bed next to Michael.

Michael moved close and spooned with Kax. He tried to go back to meditating.

Kax was more comfortable in the arms of someone, but was still having problems sleeping. She snuggled up with Michael. "Do you think there is going to be a war soon? And are we going to be on the front lines?"

Michael was almost back into his deep meditation when Kax started talking. "No, there is going to be a war. Skyler will work something out with Cane and make sure it won't be long will stop it." He lied to only to comfort Kax.

"Yeah, what is up with Skyler and his connection to Fleet Admiral Cane? Why does Skyler seem to be friends with him?"

Michael's eyes were half-open. "I don't know. Maybe it has to do with his dad. Ask him later. Now let's sleep."

Kax glanced back at Michael. He had gone back into a deep meditative trance. She hugged his arm and fell asleep.

Chapter 11

Morning soon came and Michael woke up first to see Kax in his bed. He was confused and didn't remember her being there. He checked under the covers. He was still wearing his boxers, and she was in her robe. He sighed in relief and crept out of bed, trying not to wake her. As Michael put on his pants, parts of the previous night slowly came back to him.

Stirring, Kax rubbed her eyes. "Thank you for last night. You're a wonderful guy."

Michael was zipping up his pants. He was beginning to worry he had done something wrong. "I like being a nice guy, but what did I do? I was tired and my memory is not that good when I'm in my meditative trance."

Kax got out of the bed. She brushed the hair out of her face. "I couldn't sleep and you comforted me because I was worried, that's all. Thank you so much."

Michael let out a relieved sigh and put on his shirt. "Hey, I'm a nice guy. Of course I will be there for you. Come on, let's see what Skyler's up to."

She adjusted the sash of her robe. "Ya, he is probably awake by now. Does he normally wake up this early?"

Michael shook his head. "No, he doesn't, he always sleeps in. I guess his body finally got a routine."

They both headed down to the kitchen together. The house was quiet, and the lights were off.

Kax scanned the kitchen and then headed to the stove and started working on breakfast. "I guess Skyler is still sleeping."

"He is outside on the deck." Michael pointed through the glass.

Kax's eyes bulged, and she ran to toward the glass. "Michael, go out there and make sure he is not dead."

"Will do." Michael hurried out the door and examined Skyler's cold and frozen body. He jostled his friend, trying to wake Skyler up. Michael checked his pulse. "He's just cold and sleeping."

Kax bit her lip as she hovered by the door.

Skyler slowly opened his eyes.

Michael adjusted the blanket, scooped up Skyler, and carried him over his shoulder into the house. He placed him on the couch.

Kax quickly switched on the fireplace. She handed Michael some fresh warm blankets.

"Thanks." Michael peeled off the cold ice covered blanket and wrapped Skyler in the new blanket.

Skyler opened his eyes and yawned. "What's the fuss all about? I was sleeping, y' know."

Kax rushed to Skyler's side. "You're okay! I thought you froze to near death."

Skyler shook his head. "The cold can't kill me, at least not at minus five." He leaned over and kissed Kax on the cheek. "Thanks for caring about me."

Michael squinted at the digital thermostat and told Skyler, "It's minus ten and, being out all night, you could have still frozen. You should go and get into the bath before you get hypothermia or some other illness."

Skyler grinned. "Ok. I'll go for a bath if Kax plays nurse for me."

Kax smacked Skyler on the back of his head. "He's not sick, his hot head kept him warm."

Michael walked over towards the bathroom. "I'll run your bath and call you when it is ready."

Skyler noticed Kax in her robe. "So what are you wearing under the robe?"

Kax threw a pillow at his face. "You will never know."

Michael called from down the hall, "Bath's ready!"

Skyler winked at Kax. "Next time." He got off the couch and staggered down the hall to the bathroom.

Michael whispered to Skyler as they entered the bathroom, "Can you lay off Kax for a while? This act is getting old."

Skyler took off his shirt. "Ya, I can try to do that for a bit. Anything you think will work?"

Michael rolled his eyes. "How about tonight you and I go to the bar and go chick cruising, or whatever you call it?"

Skyler patted Michael on the back. "Ah, I knew you would come around sooner or later. Now get out of here. I've got a bath to take and you don't want to see me naked."

"I'm leaving don't worry," Michael didn't hesitate to leave the room, closing the door behind him.

Skyler unzipped his pants. "You always have the chance to leave and you never do, so that's your problem."

Michael spoke through the door. "If I left every time you had a girl in the room, I would have to find a new place to live. Be thankful I don't report you for having women in the dorm after dark."

\*\*\*

Michael rejoined Kax in the kitchen. She had changed out of her robe to her daytime clothes and returned to making breakfast. "Has Skyler ever had a serious girlfriend?"

Michael sat down at the island. His brow furled, he paused. "I have no idea. I know that I have never seen him with the same girl more than twice. But I have only known him for the last three, almost four months."

She bit her lip.

"Listen, I'm going to say this once. Be careful and don't expect much from Skyler."

Kax unleashed a deep breath, trying not to think the worst about Skyler.

He checked the messages on his tablet. As soon as he turned it on the urgent alert alarm went off on his tablet. He clicked on the letter. All color drained from his face. "Kax, turn the TV on now!"

She left the plate of pancakes on the counter and rushed to the living room. "What's wrong?"

He raised his voice. "Turn the TV on now!"

He got up and ran to the living room.

Kax hurried with him to the living room and switched on the television. All the blood in her face drained as she saw the report. The news said something Michael had feared his entire life.

'Five United Galactic Forces ships were attacked. They are still gathering the survivors and death count is not certain. Families and next of kin are being notified.'

Kax turned her attention over to Michael.

His eyes had gone wide and his face white. He sat on the couch, still like a mannequin. "My father was on one of those ships."

Kax swallowed, her heart pounding. "I'll get Skyler and we can head out to the base."

Michael's sadness filled his face. "I want to go on my own but... I don't think can drive right now." He paused. "You do that. Go get him; tell him we're heading back to base."

## Chapter 12

Skyler sped down the highway with Kax on his back and Michael in the sidecar. Skyler had an idea of what Michael was going through. All of them had their uniforms since they were not sure if they would be needed for work.

Once at the base, Skyler dropped off Michael in front of the infirmary. He took the bike to the parking garage. Once the bike was parked, Skyler turned to Kax. "Let's get to the hangar, we have to fight this. I will not let these things hurt anyone."

Kax hesitated. "Listen, we're both on suspension, I don't know if my security codes will work. If there is still a battle going on up there, they will have it taken care of."

Skyler shook his head. "Kax, I know that, but we have to help, okay?" He pulled out his pocket tablet and checked the status of the attack. "According to the reports I'm getting here, there is a mothership that is heading to Earth. We need to get there."

"A fighter would not have the power to attack a mothership. They must be sending battleships for that. I have never flown something that big."

A sly grin crossed his face. "Well then, we have to get on one of those ships."

"Are you not listening? I don't know if I can fly one of those ships!" she shouted as she rushed after him.

He stopped and whirled around. "There is a first time for everything. Now it's time to be a hero."

Skyler and Kax sprinted through the halls, rushing to get to the hangar. Once there, they spotted the man who was assigning ships to the older cadets and officers. Skyler tried Kax's codes in the machine and they didn't work. He came up with another idea and typed in a few more codes. He handed Kax a print out. "Found you a ship. They are on a shortage of pilots, so you're not going on the same ship as me."

She narrowed her eyes at Skyler. "How did you get us on ships?"

Skyler grinned. "Our profiles said we were suspended from classes, not duty. So I checked in for duty. There is a shortage of pilots so your name got called. You never told me how good your grades are! You're second in the academy. These are your flight documents, take them to the ship and show them and you are cleared for flight. See you later and I wish you luck." He gave her a quick kiss on the cheek.

Kax's jaw dropped like she was about to say something, but then there was a shout from behind her.

"Petty Officer Tillion, ready for duty?"

She turned around, still stunned, "Yes? Sorry that was my first time being called that. I'm not used to it."

The commanding officer nodded. "That's quite alright, follow me."

She followed him to the ship.

Skyler inspected the itineraries and crew lists. He couldn't get his name on one; there were too many captains, first officers and other command personnel, so he looked at names similar to his own. Got it! Captain Harris, thank you. He read that Harris had not checked into his ship yet. Perfect time to rush over to the HMSS Sheldon. He got there and checked into the ship as Captain Harris. Skyler sat down in the official captain's chair.

The crew regarded at him strangely. The first officer came up to Skyler. "I am First Lieutenant Jackson, and I am wondering where Captain Harris is?"

Skyler looked up at the six-foot dark haired man. He had a short beard and wore a green uniform. He showed his tablet to the officer. "Captain Harris could not make it. It was changed to me, Captain Therris, check your chart."

The first officer shot him a glare and stood back.

Skyler leaned forward. "Pilot, are we ready for takeoff?"

The pilot turned around in his chair. "It's O'Neil, sir, Officer O'Neil, and we will be ready in about thirty seconds. Want me to start the countdown?"

"Sounds good, Officer O'Neil."

Jackson spoke up. "Sir, shouldn't you check the roster to make sure all the crew has boarded?"

Skyler quickly skimmed through the roster on his tablet. "This is an emergency situation. If you're not here on time, we leave without you." There were at least four crew members not signed in.

Jackson took his seat next to Skyler. He groaned at Skyler's unprofessionalism.

Skyler sat back in his chair and spread his legs. "O'Neil, start the countdown."

A countdown from twenty started on the view screen in front of them. Skyler flipped on the intercom. "This is Captain Therris, your acting captain. In less than twenty seconds, we will be taking off to fight these monsters and make them pay for what they have done. I want all to be ready for takeoff. Once we are in orbit, man battle stations and keep the weapons loaded."

Silence filled the room as they listened to the captain's orders. They all watched the three screens as the countdown continued. 10… 9… 8… The pilot flicked all the switches and followed the coordinates to the location. 6… 5… 4… O'Neil had his hand on the inertial damper and got ready to pull 2… 1… 0. Take off. The ship flew into orbit and headed to their destination.

Jackson turned his seat towards Skyler. "Captain Therris, I know we are in the middle of a battle, but do you think that comment about the Cassiopeians being monsters was appropriate?"

Skyler swung around in his chair to face the lieutenant. "Lieutenant Jackson, we are at war with these things, I think, as your captain, I have the right to call them whatever I want."

Jackson pinched the bridge of his nose. "You are right, Captain. You may say and name call who you want. I was suggesting you be more sensitive to the few Cassiopeian crew members we have."

Skyler gritted his teeth. "There are Cassiopeian crew members?"

Jackson nodded smugly. "Yes there are, Captain. There are a handful of them on the ship's crew and some of them work as the weapons experts. I am just saying it's not wise to use derogatory terms."

"Thank you, Lieutenant, I will issue an apology." Skyler inspected his chair's console, hit the red button and a loud alarm clanged.

The first officer leaned forward, turned off the alarm and hit the blue button. "Sorry, sir, but I think this is the button you were seeking."

Skyler leaned forward into the speaker. "This is your captain speaking. I would like to apologize for that alarm. It was a test, and to all members of the Cassiopeian race aboard, I apologize for anything that may have upset you earlier. Captain out." Skyler got comfy in his seat and looked around. He could tell the first officer didn't care for him much, and he didn't let it bother him.

The pilot twisted in his chair. "Captain, we will be approaching our destination in a few minutes."

Skyler nodded. "Thank you, Officer O'Neil. Once we arrive, I want you to get a nice clear view of the mothership, so when the torpedoes go off they can have a good clear shot."

"Aye, Captain." The pilot rotated his chair back towards the counsel.

The first officer narrowed his eyes at Skyler.

They arrived on time at the battlefield. Skyler stared at the view screen. This was the first outer space battle he had seen. Many ships were flying around and shooting at the mothership. Everything was going so fast. A few ships held on badly damaged while others were destroyed. It was not what he had imagined at all. He gulped.

*What have I gotten myself into? This was no place for a boy. That was what he was, a boy.* It took combat for him to finally see that.

He could die. He had to face his mortality. He could die without ever letting his friends and family know how he felt about them. *Is this going to be my end?* He placed his head in his hands. Even if he got out of this alive, what about Kax? He made her go. *Why couldn't I have stayed home? Why did I have to be a hero, why did I have to fight a battle that wasn't mine... or is it?* The image of Michael's face when he found out his father was in danger came to his mind.

He raised his head, remembering why he was here. It was why he made Kax go, because there were people, friends and family who were going to die. Someone had to stop them. *If it wasn't him, then who?*

The first officer clapped his hand on Skyler's shoulder and shook him a little. "Captain, sir, there is a message. The crew wants permission to attack."

Skyler snapped out of his daze and pressed his intercom. "Fire two torpedoes at the mothership head on and wait for my orders."

The torpedoes moved straight ahead to the mothership hitting it head on not making much damage or combustion off the shields of the ship. The first officer addressed Skyler. "Captain, what is the purpose of that? We wasted two torpedoes? Why didn't we fight at the open areas of the ship like the others?"

Skyler rotated in his chair. "The answer is simple, Lieutenant. A ship like that doesn't expose vulnerable spots when it has shielded capabilities. Meaning they're stronger. Let me show you." He wheeled his chair to the right side. "Pardon me, Officer Technician, please pull up the video of when the torpedoes' hit their shields and prepare for me to tell you when to pause."

"Aye, Captain," The science technician pulled up the video on the main viewer. She played the clip, and they watched the torpedoes go out shattering as they hit. Skyler snapped his fingers. "Stop."

The screen lit up with the view and the highlighted shields. "That is why, Lieutenant, look at the shield."

The lieutenant examined the screen more closely.

"Zoom in on the ship."

The science technician zoomed in close.

"This is not a real mothership. They are planning a bigger attack because why would they send a ship that has holes in its shields? Leaving parts vulnerable and having a ship that has plate shields. I noticed it when I saw another ship hit, and I saw this." He got up and pointed on the screen. "That is a seam in the plate. That is where we are going to send all our force. It will move the shields over and put a crack into their ship's hull, destroying the ship faster."

Lieutenant Jackson examined the screen. His eyebrows raised. "I must say, Captain, that is impressive."

Skyler grinned and sat back in his chair. "Communications, please send these images to the HMSS Autumn and tell them our plans. Have them notify the others."

"Aye, Captain." She followed the order and pressed the buttons to send the message. Skyler hit the intercom to the control room. "Okay, I am having coordinates sent to you and send every torpedo and any other weapons we have at this time."

He looked up. "O'Neil, send the coordinates to the control room and let's roast this ship."

"Aye, Captain," O'Neil hit a few buttons on his controls.

Their torpedoes fired one after another, and they were starting to notice the real damage to the ship. The other ships were joining in one by one. Skyler grinned. This was easy. They were going got win this. The enemy ship retreated in the fighting. His adrenaline pumping, he stood up and shouted, "Lock on to the target and do not let this ship get away. We're going to make these bastards pay!"

The bridge went silent and followed their captain's orders. Skyler noticed they were running low on torpedoes and they were down to their last two. He hit the intercom to controls and orders. "This is our last shot. Fire the two together."

The engineer spoke up. "There has to be a thirty-second delay or the torpedoes might explode. You'll have to wait, Captain."

Skyler shook his head. "We need all our force in the last attack. You have to do it this way, all the ships are running out of ammo. If we don't try this, we may not make it back."

The engineer took a deep breath. "I wish I had your faith, Captain."

Skyler held his breath as the first torpedo fired out and the other one followed right after. They didn't blow up on takeoff, but hopefully they wouldn't change speed. They watched the screen, and the mothership got further away all holding on for dear life hoping nothing went wrong. 3... 2... 1 Boom! Clear hit! The mothership's side blew up, and it had clear permanent damage to the shields. The other ships fired at the remains. The battle was over, the mothership destroyed. They could all relax.

Skyler rubbed his face and shook his head. He was happy to be alive. The entire crew celebrated behind him. He took a deep breath and turned to the pilot. "Officer O'Neil, set course for Earth."

The pilot smiled. "Aye, Captain, next stop, Earth."

## Chapter 13

Back on Earth, there are two security officers and one angry Fleet Admiral Davis waiting for the HMSS Sheldon to return to port. The ship landed at the port and the crew slowly disembarked.

Skyler was excited that he made it home alive. He couldn't wait to tell Kax and Michael how much they meant to him and be thankful he was alive. He was in his own nirvana when he stepped off the ship. Two security officer seized his hands and placed him in handcuffs and Fleet Admiral Davis said, "Cadet Therris, you are under arrest for impersonating an officer and stealing a federation starship."

Skyler took his head out of the clouds and frowned. "But I blew up the mothership. I'm a hero, and you don't arrest heroes. Who sent this order?"

The female fleet admiral glanced at her tablet. "Lieutenant Jackson put in the report and I, Fleet Admiral Davis, am making the arrest for this ship because it is part of my fleet."

Skyler didn't want to go. He knew it was a crime, but he could justify it. "I demand to see Fleet Admiral Cane. He will clear this mess up."

Fleet Admiral Davis snarled, "I'm sorry, but I can't do that right now. You have to go to the holding cell and await trial for your actions. I can send a memo to Fleet Admiral Cane to visit you later, but not now." She faced the guards and ordered, "Take him to a holding cell."

Skyler struggled to no avail. He noticed Kax in the distance, talking to her captain. He yelled out to her. "Kax! Get Cane! I'm being arrested, but I'm okay."

Kax tried to run over to Skyler, but her captain clamped his hand on her shoulder and held her back. She watched as they steered Skyler away.

***

Michael was in the infirmary, waiting to hear the news on his father. He didn't want to lose him, but right now he didn't even know what condition his father was in. This was the thing he feared most in the world. This was the one thing he never wanted to happen, at least not this soon. It was too soon for him to leave. His eyes filled with sadness. This was not how it was supposed to end.

The doctor approached Michael. "Hello, Mr. Jones. I'm Dr. Kelley and I need you to fill out some forms before we can continue with treatment. You are the next of kin, right?"

Michael nodded and accepted the tablet from the doctor. "How is he doing, Doctor? What condition is he in?"

Sorrow filled Dr. Kelley's face. "He is badly wounded and we're doing some tests so we know what is wrong. Then we are doing emergency surgery. Only time will tell how serious his condition really is."

Michael signed the tablet. "Why do you have to do tests first?"

The doctor sighed. "Mr. Jones, we think your father might have busted a few ribs on top of other things, but he is bleeding from his mouth and ears which is a sign of something worse. We have to know before he is cut open, we need to make sure it doesn't do more damage."

Michael shook his head. He almost couldn't take it to know his father was in this bad of condition and handed the tablet back to the Doctor. "Do all you can to save him. Don't let him die, dammit, he is all I have in this world and there is so much I don't know, but I don't want my father to suffer."

Dr. Kelley took the tablet. "I will do everything in my power to make sure he is alright." The doctor headed back behind the large doors.

Michael watched the doors and tried to not to think of his dad in dire conditions but couldn't shake the image. He sat down thinking of his father who stood taller than he did. His smoky brown combed back hair and his bright orange eyes. Was this the end of a great strong man? He feared the answer. He waited in the room, not sure if he would ever see his father alive again. He tried so hard to hold back the tears, because to him, tears were a sign he had given up. He wanted to stay strong so when his father did see him again it would be as if none of it had ever happened. Slowly, tears trickled down his cheeks.

Kax got to the hospital. She went over to Michael who was sitting hunched in the waiting room crying. She sat next to him and put her hand on his shoulder. "I guess it's not good news?"

Michael picked up his head and a brief smile crossed his face, but it disappeared as quickly as it came. He gave Kax a hug. "Thanks for coming. He could die, Kax. They're trying to save him, but so many things are going wrong, and fixing him might make him worse. Kax, I could lose my father."

Kax hugged Michael tightly. "You are not going to lose your father, okay? You know that they will not let it happen. He is going to walk out of here a healthy man and you will go back to doing all the things you always did together, you hear me?"

Michael tightened his arms around Kax. "I wish this never happened."

Kax rubbed his back, trying to get him to be calm. A few moments later, Michael let go of Kax and stopped crying. "Where is Skyler?"

She let out a long breath. "Would you believe me if I told you he was in jail?"

Michael shook his head and covered his face. "I turn my back for a minute and this is what I get, this is just great. Now what did he do? And should I be worried?"

Kax laughed. "No, he will be fine, I hope. He saved us all."

Michael wrinkled his brow. "What do you mean?"

"Well." Kax hesitated. "He stole a ship by changing the name on the itinerary breaking rules and, well, he might have figured out how to stop and destroy the mothership which he figured out was a decoy and there's a bigger attack coming and, well, that's about it."

Michael rolled his eyes. "He thought he could get away with that?" He paused. "But he really did the other stuff? Maybe there is some potential in him after all, but wait, if he is friends or something with Admiral Cane, why is he being arrested?"

Kax scratched her ear. "Um, well, Admiral Cane isn't in charge of that fleet, Admiral Davis is."

Michael rubbed his chin. "Fleet Admiral Davis? I didn't think she was still around. Oh, if there is one person not to get on the bad side of it's Davis, she's horrid. I know she will make Skyler pay maybe knowing Admiral Cane will help save his ass but not for long."

"I don't know what she is going to do. I need to get Cane to talk to Skyler."

Michael scoffed. "As long as she hasn't found a way to stop you."

"I still have to try." Kax stood up. "I will be back. I will go and check if I can get a hold of Cane and hopefully he can help."

Michael wanted to wait for his father, but he didn't want Skyler to get kicked out or sent to jail. He got up from his chair. "I am not letting Skyler get hurt. He saved lives and avenged my father. I owe him. My dad will be in surgery for a few more hours, I can do this."

Kax gave Michael a hug. "Well, then, we have no time to waste."


Chapter 14

The jail cell was not modern at all, with its iron bars and stone structure. Water leaked from the ceiling and walls. The bed was a board of rotting wood with a soiled blanket on top.

Dammit, what am I doing here? Skyler paced back and forth in the room. This is what a UGF jail cell looks like? I'm worried that if I touch anything I might get the plague. Civilian holding cells are better. Oh, I hope I don't have to be in here too much longer.

***

Kax and Michael headed to the fleet admiral's office and found it was busier than normal. Kax didn't pay any attention to the secretary who didn't seem to be paying attention to them and walked right by.

Fleet Admiral Cane was searching his computer for some kind of information.

Michael spoke up. "Fleet Admiral Cane, we need your help."

The fleet admiral raised his head from his computer and acknowledged Michael. "Cadet Jones and Cadet Tillion. How I may help you?"

"I'm still on suspension. It's Petty Officer Tillion." Kax's hand trembled.

The fleet admiral regarded them strangely. "What is going on? You don't get ranks like that when you're out on suspension, who gave you that rank?"

"That's what we are here about, sir. You know the attacks earlier? Michael's father was in one and is in critical condition. Skyler didn't want anything bad to happen to anyone else, and he put me on the available for duty list. He switched places with Captain Harris. And now, he is in jail, but he saved us all. He went and figured out how to defeat them and that it wasn't the real mothership."

The fleet admiral typed in a few things on his computer. "What were the names of your ships?"

"I was on the HMSS Autumn and Skyler was on the HMSS Sheldon."

The fleet admiral searched and found the recording of the black boxes and studied Skyler's work and Kax's piloting. He turned back to them. "Impressive, but I have bad news. I would personally reward this kind of brave behavior with a slight punishment. The end justifies the means and in my mind that classifies him as a hero but…"

Kax's heart raced with the fleet admiral's pause.

With a heavy sigh the fleet admiral continued. "I am not in charge of the HMSS Sheldon or HMSS Autumn. They're in Fleet Admiral Davis's fleet, not mine. That's why you were able to report for duty, because it's another fleet -- another class of cadets. She trains the officers under her by a different skill list and I do mine by experience. You are all my cadets, and I can try to get Skyler back, but Fleet Admiral Davis is one who is hard to negotiate with."

Michael took a deep breath. "Is there anything we can do?"

The fleet admiral shook his head. "I wish there was, Cadet Jones. If I find anything I will let you know, but this is not a case where a character reference is going to cut it." He turned his attention towards Kax. "Oh, and Kax? Thank you for your service. You will be rewarded with Skyler and then both of you are off suspension. I will need you to stay near your phones, then I will let you know if you are needed. Any more questions?"

They checked with each other and shook their heads. Michael addressed the fleet admiral. "I'm not sure it is my place to ask, but I have noticed that, in the last few months, you and Cadet Therris seem to be closer than you are with most cadets?"

The fleet admiral smiled. "Skyler didn't tell you? I have no problem telling you the basics of the story. I was his father's first officer, and we were very close. I was also close to his mother. It's more like I'm an unofficial step-father or uncle kind of thing. That isn't why he gets away with things but that is one reason I watch out for him. I made a promise to his father to protect him if anything happened to his dad. Any more questions, feel free to ask Skyler, that boy needs to open up. Now you two have got to be off. I have to deal with one of the two people I hate to work with."

"Just curious, sir. Who is the other person?" Kax asked.

Cane rubbed his temple. "Skyler's mother."

Michael and Kax saluted the fleet admiral and headed out for the office.

"Hey, Michael I will meet you at the dorm later. I want to go talk to Skyler."

"Sounds good to me. I'll see you later."


Chapter 15

Kax headed down to the UGF prison. There were two guards in front of Skyler's cell. In the cell, she could see Skyler pacing back and front. She approached the cell. One of the guards in his black and yellow security uniform came forward.

"Stop, what is your business here?" he demanded in a deep booming voice.

"I wanted to visit the prisoner."

The guard waved over the other guard. "My partner needs to pat you down if you want to stay."

"That's fine with me." Kax lifted her arms at the side and the other male guard came over and gave her a quick pat down.

"She's clean." The guard stepped away. "She can stay."

"Is it possible to have some privacy with the prisoner or do you two have to be here?"

They looked at each other. "We will stand by the outside door. There is only one way out of here so don't get any ideas." They left the room.

She walked up to Skyler in the cell.

Skyler greeted her with a smile. "Kax, why are you here?"

"I wanted to see you. I feel bad you are stuck here in this cell and I'm not."

He grinned. "So, you're here for a conjugal visit?"

Kax glared at him. "Not in the slightest. I meant I committed a crime too, and they didn't arrest me. We both broke the rules."

Skyler shook his head. "You didn't commit a crime. I said we were not suspended from duty I just put you on a ship that was short a pilot. I am the one who impersonated an officer. You are innocent."

"Oh! That makes more sense now. You know Davis is going to throw the book at you."

"Cane will protect me. I did what I felt was right and saved the day I'll take my punishment."

She rolled her eyes. "Why are you so reckless? Don't you care that your career is at stake!"

Skyler walked over to the piece of steel bed and sat down. "I'm confident I won't lose my career over this. And not because of Cane but because in the end I did the right thing. Like my dad used to say, 'Be a hero and it won't matter what damage is done.'"

"I bet your dad wouldn't have done something so reckless!"

Skyler scoffed. "He did a lot worse but back when he was captain there wasn't a lot of rules saying what you can and can't do. He is the reason there are so many regulations today."

She sat down on the cold cement floor. "Skyler, one thing that has been bugging me since we got suspended. Why do you have so many boxes under your bed?"

Skyler rubbed his face. "That's all my stuff. I don't have a home to go to. The forces is my home now."

"But I thought only your father died? Don't you have a mother?"

Skyler rolled his eyes. "Technically yes. But I have not talked to her since I turned sixteen." He let out a long sigh. "Let me start at the beginning. My dad died when I was five. My mother began seeing Cane, but he was always working so he would be by for no more than a week at a time. My mom never paid attention to me. She was always working, and the school wasn't far from my house so she would wake me up and then take off. She would take me shopping once a year on my birthday... well, around my birthday, she didn't always remember. Cane was there for me more. When I was twelve, she said she was done with Cane and quickly married her old high school sweetheart Charles. He hates me. He was around more and whenever he felt like it he would beat me. My mother never believed me and always took his side."

Kax's face drooped. "That's horrible, I am so sorry."

Skyler laughed. "My story gets worse. I found reasons to not come home unless my mother was there. I joined the lacrosse team and at age fourteen I lost my virginity, and soon after I started drinking and going to parties. I was always in trouble for something in school. I spent most of the time when I was home hiding in the attic reading my dad's old journals and books, that's how I know so much. Finally, when I was sixteen, Charles found out about my drinking and beat me so bad he cracked three of my ribs and gave me this scar." He got up and approached Kax. He lifted his cadet jacket and showed a three-inch scar on the right side of his ribs.

Kax reached out and lightly touched the scar. "Oh, my, that's awful. Did you report it?"

Skyler shook his head and put down his shirt. "No, because Charles Roux is a governor and no one will believe the disgruntled stepson. He then pulled out his gun and told me to get out and threated to shoot me if I ever came back. So I ran. I went to my girlfriend's house and she let me use the phone to call my uncle Justin. He picked me up and let me stay with him. I tried to get a hold of my mother a few times but Charles intercepted the messages so I have not talked to her since. When I was eighteen, I moved out with what remained of my stuff. My uncle was able to go and collect my things. And now I live here on base. I've got nowhere else to go."

Tears came to her eyes. She reached in through the bars and gave Skyler a hug. "I'm so sorry, I had no idea."

He hugged her back. "It's not something I talk about. You and my uncle are the only ones who know the full story."

Kax broke the hug. "If this is all you have why are you so reckless then?"

Skyler smiled and got up. "Because I know what I am doing and I have a plan. This cell wasn't part of my plan but I'll figure something out. But it's getting late you should go and get some sleep. I'll be here trying not to catch the plague."

Kax stood up and saw the light in the window had gone black. "I guess you're right. It is late and I should be getting back. I'll see you in the morning." She leaned in and gave Skyler a kiss on the cheek.

His eyes widened. "What was that for?"

She winked. "For good luck." She fixed her skirt and left the room.

***

Kax knocked on Michael's door. He opened the door in his uniform pants and black tank top. "Hey, Kax, how is Skyler doing?"

"He will be fine." She peeked in through the door. "Can I come in?"

Michael stepped back from the door. "Please come in, I was just about to head out and visit my dad but I was just resting till you came."

"As long as I'm not disturbing you." She entered the room, surveying it, and noted a bed half made with lots of clothes around it, along with a box of condoms on the desk. She laughed at the bed. "So let me guess. This one's Skyler's."

Michael pointed at his pressed sheets made to a tee and no clothes on the floor. "Is it that obvious?" He shifted his head around.

"Hey, I'm going to change out of my uniform. Do you mind turning around?"

"Oh, sure, no problem." Kax went over, sat on Skyler's bed, and faced the wall. "Why do I miss him? I can't stand him most of the time and now I want him here."

Michael changed out of his uniform to civilian clothes. "I don't know, but I kind of miss him too. What did you talk about?"

Kax lay on the bed. "Just some stuff about his parents. He is not as big of a jerk as I thought."

"You can turn around now." Michael was now wearing a pair of blue jeans and red t-shirt. "Ya, Skyler has layers."

Kax rolled over on the bed. "So you're heading back to the hospital?" She yawned.

"Ya, you can stay here if you want?"

Kax hugged a pillow. "Thanks. I think I will have a nap, it's been a long day, and I know you're worried about your dad. Make sure you get some sleep tonight."

"I will and if I were you, I would not look in the third drawer. Skyler gets worse."

Her eyes narrowed at drawer. "Don't worry I won't, and I wish you and your father the best."

Michael headed to the door. "Thanks for everything."

After he left, Kax lay in the bed thinking. So Skyler's dad was my mother's captain. I wish my dad would have told me more about her. I'll have to ask Skyler what he knows. He might not be such a bad guy after all. She crawled under the covers. Wow, this bed is comfier than mine. Maybe I am just tired.

***

At the hospital, Michael was in the waiting room awaiting word about his father. He tugged on his hair, I wish there was something I could do. I hate being this powerless. He put his hands together in prayer. "Please, God, don't let anything happen to my father." He paused. I can't lose faith. I need it more than ever.

Dr. Kelley stepped out of the operating room. "Um, I'm not interrupting you am I?"

Michael lowered his hands. "No. Please, Doctor, what is the news?"

"Your father is in stable condition. You can come in and see him if you would like, Mr. Jones."

Michael's eyes lit up. "Really, Doctor, is he okay?"

Dr. Kelley skimmed his chart. "He survived surgery, he is waking up and you can see him, but we are waiting to see how he does over the next twenty-four hours."

Michael got up and followed Dr. Kelley to the room where his father lay.

Dr. Kelley switched off the force field door and headed into the room.

Michael saw his father laying on the bed, hooked up to tubes and machines. He held back the tears. Never had he seen his father in this condition before. He rushed to the right side of his father's bed. His eyes were closed. His skin was pale and his cheeks were sunken in. He could not hold back the tears anymore and began to cry. Dr. Kelley came closer to Michael. "You can stay here if you want, he should be waking up soon."

Michael glanced at the doctor. "Thank you for all you have done. It means a lot to me."

Dr. Kelley rested his hand on Michael's shoulder. "I was glad to help." Dr. Kelley walked out of the room leaving Michael to have some alone time.

Michael waited there at his father's side. He couldn't stop crying.

His father soon opened his eyes and noticed his son. "Michael, you can stop crying, I'm going to be okay."

Michael smiled to his father. "Dad, there you are. I didn't know if you would be okay, I am so happy that you are alive."

Sam gave his son a slight grin. "I'm a lot stronger than you think. I am glad you are here."

Michael couldn't stop smiling. There were so many things he wanted to say and ask, but he was distracted because of the relief that his father was going to be okay. He wiped the tears away from his eyes. "I was so worried you were going to die."

Sam put his hand on his son's head. "Well, I am alive now and you don't have to worry about anything."


Chapter 16

As dawn broke, Kax heard her phone ring. She woke up and answered it, half-awake. "Hello?" Her eyes were half-open. It was Fleet Admiral Cane.

"Cadet Tillion, we're going to need you to be at the courthouse in an hour. Can you make it? In dress uniform."

Kax's eyes opened, and she jumped up in the bed. "Yes, sir, I can be there. What about Michael?"

"I will be calling Cadet Jones in a bit."

She scurried out of bed. "Sounds good. Do you want me to make sure Skyler has his dress uniform?"

The fleet admiral paused for a second. "If you can bring it, do so. But I don't think there will be time for it."

Kax smiled. "Got it. Thank you, sir."

"Good, I will be off, see you in an hour."

Kax rushed back to her room waved to her roommate and quickly grabbed her dress uniform. "Been real busy, I'll talk to you later, I'm kind of in a hurry.

She left before anything more could be said. She ran down the halls while calling Michael's phone. "Hey, Michael, I got your message, where are you? I have your uniform. Where do you want me to meet you?"

"Courthouse is fine. I have to fill out some more paperwork and then I will be heading down there."

Kax smiled and kept going. "Okay, sounds good, and tell your dad I wish him well."

"You can tell him yourself later when you see him. He's better now. But we have to worry about Skyler."

Kax slowed down her pace. She tried to catch her breath. "You are right, that is the important thing right now."

"I'll be there."

Kax hung up and hurried to the courthouse. Once inside, she went into the bathroom and changed quickly into her purple satin dress uniform. It was similar to her cadet uniform dress but satin, with the officer's fold over the chest flap. Once she was dressed, she returned to the hall and waited for the others to show up.

The fleet admiral showed up shortly after. She approached him.

"Hello, Cadet Tillion. I'm glad you could make it."

She stood at attention. "I wouldn't miss this for the world." She shuffled the hangers in her hands and extended Skyler's uniform. "I brought his uniform. Is there time to get it to him? I know you said you weren't sure."

The fleet admiral took the uniform. "I just got here. I haven't seen him, but I will see if I can get it to him before. It's not mandatory if he doesn't have it due to the circumstances, but it is nice. I don't think this will be a long trial, anyway."

Kax nodded. "I'm worried about Skyler, he a great guy and one of my only friends."

The fleet admiral smiled. "You remind me of your mother when you talk like that."

Kax locked her surprised gaze on the fleet admiral. "Really? You think I'm like my mother?"

The fleet admiral shot her a friendly smile. "You're very much like her. Your mother was our pilot. She was amazing. I have never seen a pilot as good as her. She had a heart of gold and always put others before herself."

She blushed. "I didn't know, she died when I was little. But I like hearing stories about her."

"You can come by my office anytime and ask about her. I have lots of stories to tell."

They smiled at each other for a bit then heard the click clack of Fleet Admiral

Davis's heeled boots. Cane spun around and saw Davis. She frowned at Cane. "Your cadet is guilty and is going to get kicked out for this, you know."

Cane took a deep breath and straightened his back. "My cadet is a hero. He saved many lives and many of them were your cadets and officers. If I were you, I would not be kicking out a man of great expectations."

Davis laughed sharply. "You think your cadet has potential? He needs to be disciplined. Something he must not be getting from you."

Cane snarled back. "Say that again and I will point out all your cadets failed to see what Skyler saw, and that you lost four ships."

Michael came running down the halls and stopped when he got to Kax. He was trying to catch his breath. He looked around and saw the two fleet admirals. Quickly he saluted.

She glanced at Michael then at Cane. "See, discipline is all that is needed. And this cadet knows it."

"You're confusing obedience with discipline. Discipline discourages creative thinking, and that is what wins wars."

Michael slanted his eyebrows at Kax.

She handed him his uniform. She whispered to Michael, "I'll tell you about it later, just get changed."


*** 


"Hey, no shoving!" Skyler snapped at the security officers as they brought him to the room to see Fleet Admiral Cane.

"Well, stop struggling," The dark-haired security officer replied.

"You can let him go, he is fine." Cane spoke up from behind the table.

The security officers removed the handcuffs from Skyler and left the room.

Cane placed Skyler's dress uniform on the table. "We don't have much time, I asked Fleet Admiral Thompson for this time to brief you on the case."

Skyler rubbed his wrists and scanned the tiny 5x5 powder blue room. There was a small wooden table with two basic chairs. "I thought this was an open and shut case. Is there anything else I should be worried about?"

Cane slid the uniform over to him. "It should be but this time is mostly for you to get changed and go over the details."

Skyler lifted off his cadet jacket and took his dress uniform jacket out of the bag. He went to unzip his pants. "Um, Cane can you turn around or close your eyes? I didn't mind the top because of my tank top but um I don't have anything on under these." He pointed to his pants.

"You really should wear underwear, it can save your life. But it is not required." Cane faced the wall. "You realize Davis is going to throw the book at you?"

"Do you think Davis scares me?" Skyler finished getting dressed and sat down in the other seat.

Cane faced Skyler. "You should be afraid. If it weren't for me, you would have already been thrown out. But I know you did the right thing even if you did break the rules and you will be punished for that and this will go against your record."

Skyler rubbed his temples. "How far will this set me back on being a captain?"

"Not too far. You are lucky this happened in your first year. You can make up for this in the coming years if you keep a good clean record from now on this will practically disappear. But when you are up there, I need you to listen. Only speak when spoken to and do not make any outbursts, do you understand?"

Skyler let out a deep sigh. "Ya, I know. I understand, I just wish I could get this all over with."

"It will all be over soon. Just relax." Cane went over to the door and knocked. "You can come in now."

The security officers entered the room.

Cane collected the cadet uniform. "I will see you on the stand. And remember speak only when spoken to."

Skyler nodded. "Yes, sir."

\*\*\*

The court was about to start. Kax and Michael were sitting in the front row of the silver pews. All three fleet admirals were up at the front, behind their silver metal benches facing the courtroom. The security officers ushered Skyler to the podium in the center of the room. Lieutenant Jackson was at the silver table next to Skyler. The case was ready to begin.

Skyler's heart raced. Stay calm, everyone is here for you. He had the support of his friends. I thought I was prepared for this but… what if I screw up?

The trial began, and all rose. Cane on the right, Davis on the left and Thompson in the center. Thompson took a seat, and the rest followed. Thompson read over the files. "Cadet Therris, you stand accused of impersonating an officer, theft and disobeying orders. How do you plead?"

Skyler inhaled a deep breath. I'm not giving up. He stood at attention. "Not guilty."

Thompson wrote something down. He changed focus to Lieutenant Jackson. "I have viewed the tapes of the events, so all I need from you is your answer to this question. Do you think Cadet Therris is guilty of the charges since you were there to witness these events?"

Lieutenant Jackson gazed straight at Fleet Admiral Thompson. "No, he is a hero and I am not aware of his orders but I believe this school stands for doing what is right even if it is not what was asked."

Thompson examined the file again. "I have read both statements by Fleet Admiral Cane and Fleet Admiral Davis. Since this case involves two fleet admirals, it is my place as the third admiral to make the decision, and my verdict is..."

The room went silent, and all eyes fixed on Fleet Admiral Thompson.

Skyler's heart raced. This is it. The next words that come out of his mouth will decide my fate. He clenched his fists.

The fleet admiral continued his speech. "I find Cadet Therris not guilty. Cadet Therris, you have shown great bravery, and I thank you for your efforts. I am letting you go because you are a hero not a criminal. But you are put on probation. So, no breaking anymore rules and you are not allowed to go near Davis' fleet for the rest of the year, understood?"

Skyler let out a deep sigh of relief and unclenched his fists. Yes, I'm free. "That is understood. Thank you, Your Honor, I will do my best to make this school proud."

Thompson smiled. "That is what I like to hear but no more bending the rules and you won't have to be back here, understood?"

"Yes, Your Honor. I will do my best and not break any rules."

Thompson banged his gavel. "Case dismissed."

They all got out of their seats and headed down the hall.

Kax and Michael gave Skyler a big hug.

"Oh, Skyler, we are so happy that you are alright," Kax exclaimed.

Michael patted Skyler on the head. "Dude, don't do that again, okay? I mean, come on. What am I going to do without you?"

Skyler laughed. "Glad you guys missed me, I sure missed you two last night. I especially missed you, Kax. But thank you for your visit."

"You know Kax missed you so much last night that she slept in your bed."

Skyler raised his eyebrows and smirked. "Is this so? How do I get you back into my bed?"

Kax pushed him away. "You never change, do you?"

He laughed a little. "You're the one who was sleeping in my bed."

# Chapter 17

Skyler, Kax, and Michael showed up at the hospital wearing their civilian clothes. Michael led them to his father's room. His father was lying in bed, his face paler than when Michael had last seen him.

Skyler waved to Sam. "Hello, Mr. Jones. How you are doing today? Nice to see you again."

Sam waved as much as he could. "I'm glad you are safe. I knew they wouldn't do anything to you."

Skyler brushed his hair back. "Ya, it was nothing. They can't keep a good guy down."

Sam fixed his attention on Kax. "You must be the lovely Kax. It is so nice to meet you. My son has told me lots about you."

Kax blushed. "That's nice to know, he has told me lots about you as well."

The nurse came into the room and noticed the group. "Oh, Mr. Jones, I didn't know you had visitors I will come back later."

Sam shook his head. "No, you can do your thing, my son and his friends don't mind."

The nurse went over to the bed. "It is a simple blood test. I needed to get a sample." She took a needle out and drew some blood from the IV.

Skyler watched the nurse. "Hey, could I get you to check out this cut? I got it last night in the jail cell and I think I might have gotten the plague?" Skyler rolled up the sleeve on his t-shirt and showed the nurse the cut on his arm.

She finished with the tablet and examined Skyler's arm from a distance. The blood finished drawing, "I don't think you have the plague but when I am done with taking this sample. I can take you to the doctor."

Skyler grinned. "Alright."

She finished collecting all the samples he needed and checked off a few things on his tablet. She checked over the chart again. "Looks like I'm done here. The doctor will be back later with the results."

She directed her attention to Skyler. "If you will please follow me, I will take you to see Dr. Kelley."

Skyler smiled and waved to Sam. "See you later. I'm going to get tested for the plague."

Sam turned to his son. "He does know the plague has been extinct for over 200 years?"

Michael laughed. "I'm not sure. This is why I don't like him reading books."

***

Skyler walked down the hall with the nurse. On his way, he saw an attractive nurse and stretched his neck to watch her as they passed. "Hello, Nurse." He whistled.

The first nurse led him into a room. "Wait here, the doctor will be here soon."

Skyler sat on the table and waited for the doctor.

Dr. Kelley came back a little while later. He pulled out his tablet. "Full name and birth date?"

Skyler sat up. "Skyler Logan Therris, May 21th, 130."

Dr. Kelley examined the cut on Skyler's arm. "So, you want to be a captain? That's interesting."

Skyler smiled. "It's my dream to be a Capitan. My father was one and I want to be one too."

Dr. Kelley examined the cut and saw that it was a scratch, but pressed a needle into Skyler's arm then to test his blood. "So, you joined the United Galactic Forces because your father said to?"

Skyler shook his head, barely noticing the needle. "My father died when I was a child. I joined because I wanted an adventure."

Dr. Kelley smiled. "Really? I usually see kids in here saying they are following their parents, so why do you want to be a captain? That's, like, the hardest job. So much pressure."

Skyler grinned, and the doctor waited for the blood test strip to show the result. "I don't mind it. I was captain for a bit yesterday, but that was just to save the day. When you're on the ship, you feel as if time stands still, and the captain has the support of his crew. There is nothing to fear. It's peaceful when you are there in your own world, no one to tell you how to run your life, and there's a sense of community because you all support each other in whatever is needed.

Like a family. But not like your real family that you can't stand anymore."

They both laughed at the last comment. The doctor checked the blood, and the results came up negative. "Good news, Cadet, your blood is fine. You don't have any diseases. I'll put some antiseptic on the wound to stop infection.

Dr. Kelley started to get the alcohol wipe. "I'm glad you're going on an adventure and are happy about it. I have always wanted to, but it then didn't seem right for me. I'm too old to do it now."

Skyler looked at the doctor, puzzled. "What do you mean, too old? You're never too old especially with humans living longer and longer."

"You know, I never thought of it like that. I know I am a member of the Galactic Forces, but I'm a ground doctor and I went with it because I was a doctor. They offered me a contract, but really, I thought once I finished med school half my life was gone." Dr. Kelley rubbed a wipe on Skyler's wound.

Skyler flinched when the alcohol touched his cut. "Dude, if you have even a couple of years on this earth left, it is never too late to have an adventure."

The doctor smiled. "Once again, I never thought of it like that." He came to the front of Skyler. "You are good to go. You don't have any illnesses and I cleaned up the wound, so it will not get infected."

Skyler unrolled his sleeve. "Thank you, Doctor."

Dr. Kelley escorted Skyler out of the room. "No, thank you, Mr. Therris."

Skyler was puzzled but shrugged it off. He rejoined his friends, and he threw his arms in the air. "I'm cured of the plague. I had the plague, and he cured me, but you all should get tested."

Michael rolled his eyes and turned to his dad. "This is what I have to put up with every day."


## Chapter 18


The days went back to normal. Midterm exams were coming up, and that meant more studying for all of them.

Michael's father was still in the hospital, but it didn't interfere with his schoolwork. Michael might have been at the top of his class, but he wanted to stay there.

Skyler didn't think he had to. He knew how to be a captain, and that was all that mattered.

Kax was still clinging to her friends. She wanted extra time to try out the ship simulator. She had to know it all; if she failed a test in a special division, she could be kicked out.

Skyler entered the room and saw that Michael was not back. He had the room to himself and wondered what he should do. He didn't feel like calling any of the girls that he had been with in the past. And he wasn't in the mood to find a new one. There were lots of girls who wanted to be with him, but there was only a few he wanted. One of them was in the other wing. He liked Kax; he wasn't going to deny it. He knew no women could resist him, so she had to like him, too. But she said no every time. What could he do? He could go over to her room and see how she was doing, but she would more than likely turn him away. He thought about Kax in her cute slit mini skirt and tight leggings, which drove him wild. Her strawberry blonde hair offset her royal purple uniform. He imagined unzipping her top and flipping up her skirt and doing so many things to her. He laid on the bed, feeling himself and imagining her body, rubbing his body and unzipping his pants. In his mind, she was his fantasy and could be anything he wanted. In his mind, she wanted him. He rubbed and rubbed, feeling a sense of ecstasy. He closed his eyes and he could see her pleasing him. It was going so well–he was almost there and he heard the door open. He jumped up in the bed and covered himself.

Kax walked in. "Hey, how you doing? I thought I would hang out with you after class."

Skyler could not wipe the smile from his face. "I'm glad. I would love to hang out with you." He ruffled the blankets around.

Kax glanced at Skyler and the blanket and made a disgusted face. "You know, I was going to give you a chance, but after this? No way."

Skyler stared at her. "You were going to give me a chance?"

Kax scoffed. "Yup, but now that I found you with your pants down there is no chance."

Skyler zipped his pants up under the blanket. "They're up now. Will you give me another chance?"

Kax laughed. "No way."

"You know this is a normal human thing, right?"

She shook her head. "That doesn't mean I want to know when you do it."

Michael then came into the room and saw what was going on. "Dude, did she catch you with your pants down?"

His jaw dropped. "They weren't down."

Michael covered his face. "You have to learn to keep that thing in your pants."

Kax's face mottled bright red. "So, what's everyone's exam schedule like? Mine start tomorrow."

Michael checked his tablet. "Mine also start tomorrow, but I only have to write three."

"Well, if Kax doesn't want to hang out with me I'm going for a shower. I'll be back later." Skyler got up and grabbed his towel and bathroom kit from the foot of the bed.

Michael went over to his bed. "I'm sorry about Skyler."

Kax laughed. "You're always apologizing for Skyler, it's so funny."

"I think you're right about that. For some reason, I feel like I have to apologize for him."

Kax sat on Skyler's bed. "You don't have to. He is going to be immature forever and you know it. You're the one who is mature."

Michael rolled his eyes. "That's true. So, are you nervous about your exams?"

Kax shook her head. "I have been booking in extra hours with the simulator so I can reassure myself that I know what I am doing. But I wish I could get them over with."

"I might know the stuff, but for me it means getting closer to graduating–closer to the front lines."

Her smile faded. "Well, the war hasn't officially started. Maybe if you ask the fleet admiral nicely he will let you finish in seven years instead of the four."

Michael sighed. "Maybe, but who knows? I mean it is a good idea, but not too good, because they really might need me."

"We will figure something out. See if you can get a simple trade route until it's over. We have a powerful connection now with Skyler."

Michael groaned. "I keep forgetting to talk to Skyler about that. I can't believe he never told us about that. I mean I'm not like 'hey, let's use him for connections,' but let's at least talk to him about this so we know what is going on. Do you think that's why he acts the way he does?"

"Naw, he's just immature. If he really wanted to use his connections to get somewhere, he would be worse than he is now." She tossed her hair back, "I think he just doesn't want anyone to know. But what I want to know more about is his father. He was my mother's captain, that's kind of neat. I know my mom was gone a lot, so she never told me much and I know she was in love with her captain. She and my dad used to fight about it…" She paused and disgust came over her face. "You don't think Skyler and I are brother and sister, do you? That would be just gross."

Michael laughed. "Lots of crew members fall for their captains, it's a power thing. And no I don't think you are. You could just ask your dad."

"You're probably right. I should call my dad, I haven't talked to him much since I joined the forces."

"Are you ready for your exams?"

Kax shook her head. "I might have the skills, but I don't feel ready."

Michael let out a long sigh. "Same here, I could do Skyler's in my sleep, I have been reading his books and helping him study. But mine—even if I read mine again, I don't feel I could do it, or maybe I just don't want to do it."

"I'm confused. You love the command work, but you are in the engineering division. Why is that?"

"It's because I'm a Squallite. My race might have been one of the first on Earth and one of the most useful. But we have very little rights here. We are third-rate citizens and are not allowed to be in the United Galactic Forces. So, because the humans think we are only good at electrical, they let us be engineers. And because we are considered low class citizens, there aren't many jobs for us outside of the forces either." He rubbed his face. As if exams were not stressful enough he had to be reminded of his bane. "I am grateful that this year I got Skyler as a roommate. I can use his textbooks to read when he is not and do the practice tests, and then if they ever change the laws, I am ahead. I want to be a captain. That's my dream, but so many things are holding me back."

Kax sat down next to Michael on the bed. She slipped her arm around him. "I'm sorry about that. Do you wish you were human?"

Michael rested his head on her shoulder. "No, I am happy to be myself, because humans don't change. I am more annoyed my race isn't fighting for change. I know things are different here than on our home world, but it's not fair. All the Squallites in my class have studied and learned from their parents, so we all are top of the class. There is no competition. It's like why do they even bother training us."

"Aren't their non-Squallite engineers?"

"Yes, there is but only about five out of a hundred which does add competition. But to the others, not us Squallites."

Kax sighed. "That's got to suck. We're all diverse in my division, so even if you know what you are doing, it is difficult learning how to pilot a ship. It sucks. I mean, I love flying but they're just simulations so that we cadets don't die. It's not the same. I hope they send me to the advanced classes so I can graduate early."

Michael rolled his eyes. "I wish I could get into the advanced classes, but when the class average is 95 percent there is no advance which means year four you graduate or get sent to missions for a few years on basic routes."

"Can't you transfer to the special division to extend your training?"

"Yes, I can but I don't want to, I want to be a Capitan. So, I am going to stay here until the law is changed. I would love to stop being a cadet and get paid, but the war is coming, making money sounds less worth it."

Kax nodded. "You're right, I hope nothing bad happens to you, but good news. With the medal Skyler got you, they will give you a promotion, so you can get more money and hope for a higher rank. Maybe you won't be on the front."

He contemplated that thought. "I guess you're right. They don't throw the high ranks into the front lines."

"I am in for the full seven, unless I prove I'm advanced, but we already mentioned that."

Michael laughed and got up. "Come on, let's head out to an after-hours study hall."

Kax frowned. "That's weird, you really want to do an after hours' study hall? If Skyler was here, he would have said 'that would mean staying in the room.'"

Michael and Kax busted into laughter.

\*\*\*

Michael was the only one alert for his exams and finished them in almost record time. Michael was questioning if he had made the right choices with his career. Engineering seemed too boring; he wanted adventure. His newfound friends had given his life purpose and meaning and he didn't know if he could accomplish his goals if he was in the place he was right now. He couldn't be a captain, but maybe he could bend the rules to try to get into another division.

But would that solve his problem? Was this about his career or was it something else? His life had taken a 360 in the last few months. Was he the same man? What was he going to do? Being bored was not the answer. These questions danced in his head.

Kax was a little tired from a long night of studying. But she finally felt confident enough to do her exams in her sleep. Soon, she was about to find out if the work paid off. Kax didn't know where her life was going either. She was torn between two men who liked her and she liked them too; they were her friends. Her grades were suffering a bit because of them. She wanted to get her mind off men, which was tough as all her roommate could think of was men. She was like a female Skyler and it was driving Kax nuts. But there was no man in Kax's life. She had men, but not a man. Maybe she needed an attractive male who was more than just a friend. It could be the distraction she needed to get back on track. She smiled. When exams were over, she would go drinking with Skyler to find someone for herself.

The morning arrived and so did exams.

Skyler went to his exams wearing his sunglasses, hungover. He wore the glasses until the commodore told him to take them off. Skyler was happy with his exams; no stress at all. Hangover or not he had it all under control. This was the time of his life to excel and have a party. He loved the United Galactic Forces and joining was the first time in his life he felt he was in control. He wanted the schooling part to be over. He knew he could be captain and wanted to be one more than anything. He was now one step closer. But it was steps he felt that were impossible to finish.

Once done with the exams they all met up in the cafeteria. They got their food and sat together.

Kax picked at her food. "What do you think they put in the spaghetti?"

"Artificial vitamins and sawdust."

Skyler gobbled down his and frowned at Michael with his eyes wide. "Ew, that's gross. Why tell me something like that?"

Michael slid his plate over to Skyler. "Here, you can eat my food. Then I'm going to go to the city to get real food."

Kax and Skyler exchanged glances and then scrambled to their feet in unspoken agreement.

"Wait for us," Kax said.


Chapter 19


They took Michael's bike, and they drove an hour until they hit the city limits. There, they searched for a real whole food restaurant, not one of the replicated fast-food places. They eventually found a place called Leida's. There were twelve people ahead of them.

Leida's was an old-fashioned style restaurant with dark hardwood plank floors and a white stucco ceiling. There were booths along the wall, the booths were black and made to look like they were from the last century. There was a long bar on the back wall next to the hallway to the kitchen.

Kax stared at the line clustered around the door. "Damn, we're not going to get a table here now."

Skyler put on a crafty grin. "I have never had to wait for a table in my life, just watch me." He surveyed the restaurant floor. He spotted a table for four where there were three people sitting. He left the line and went over to them. "Hello, there. You seem like nice people. My girlfriend and I are celebrating our anniversary. Silly me, I forgot to make a reservation. You know how young love is. I was wondering if you kind people would like to give us your table."

A guy and two girls were sitting together. The guy glowered at Skyler. "No way we're giving you this table, it's ours. We stood our turn in line and you can too."

Skyler sniffled, and a tear came to his eye. "Aw, really, I'm sorry to bother you, I really wouldn't mind waiting. But this is the table me and my girlfriend sat in on our first date and I was trying to make it special."

The brunette at the table nudged the dark-haired guy. "Come on, give him the table. He wants it more."

The guy frowned at Skyler. "Listen, buddy, I waited for this table and if I were you, I would do the same."

Skyler sighed, drew out his wallet and took out a hundred dollar bill. "Is this enough?"

The guy grinned when he saw the money. "Make it three, and you got a deal. One for each."

Skyler gave him the money, and all three got up and left. Skyler took a seat and waved his friends over.

The waitress came with three drinks and placed them on the table. "Oh, you're not the ones who were in here, what happened to them?"

Skyler grinned. "They got a bad case of fat wallet is all, but we will keep their drinks, did they order or do we get to see menus?"

The waitress smiled. "Okay, I will be right back with your menus."

Michael looked at Skyler. "So how much did you pay the guy?"

Skyler smirked as he took a sip from his drink. "You don't want to know. Be happy you are here and I have money left over to pay."

Kax giggled. "Oh good. I thought you were going to tell me you told them I was your girlfriend and that it was our anniversary."

Skyler stretched back. "Ok, I didn't."

The waitress then came by with the menus. "I'll be back in a minute to take your order."

Skyler flirted with the waitress with his eyes.

They all read their menus and thought about what they are going to order.

Michael peered over at Skyler. "So what kind of budget are we looking at here?"

Skyler lifted his eyes up from his menu. "Don't worry about the price. You can order a dessert or two, or five."

Michael figured out what he wanted and put his menu down.

The waitress came back and saw all their menus were down. "Ok everyone so what would you like to order?"

Skyler flashed a smile. "I would like the gorgon stir fry."

"I'll have the Centauri squash."

Michael finished off with, "And I'll have the Galaxy salad."

The waitress wrote out their orders. "Sounds good. I'll pass this order to the chef and I will be back soon."

Skyler flirted again with his eyes at the blonde thin waitress.

"Skyler, you are pathetic. You really think you're going to hook up with the waitress?"

Skyler smirked. "Hook up, maybe get us free drinks? Yes."

Michael rolled his eyes. "You know what, I don't care. All I care about is that I will be eating whole foods again. Been off my diet for too long."

Kax narrowed her eyes at Michael. "You need to diet?"

He shook his head. "No, it's a Squallite thing."

Skyler noticed the waitress wave to him. "I'll be right back, folks."

\*\*\*

Michael and Kax sat there across from each other. Kax admired the style of the restaurant and smiled. "This is a nice place they have. The theme they have going on has really captured the early 2000 period."

"I guess the old styles are coming back. It's so weird this place would have been cool and new around 2013, but being 2218, it's just rustic."

Kax lowered her brow. "2218 are you talking about CE? Because the earth goes by the Golden Age calendar now so its 148 GA?"

Michael shook his head. "You're right, sorry about that I got confused."

Kax was still frowning. "What do you mean no one uses CE no more it's no longer the Common Era we are now in the Golden Age so it's all GA I'm surprised you still know the other calendar why is that?"

Michael shrugged. "Don't want you to think less of me, but my family are Gregorian Catholics."

"You still believe in God? That's so weird. No one does, he died."

Michael sighed. "I don't believe that. He is an entity that is in all of us, and the world was better when we had faith."

Kax watched the admiration in Michael's eyes. Wow Michael is so sexy when he talks about something he is passionate about. Makes it hard to choose between him and Skyler. "It's nice, come to think of it that way. I mean, yes, it caused wars, but so many people now live without hope. They think of life as just today, and there is nothing in the end. It's all black. Some might see it as a chance to leave a mark, but why leave a mark if you can't enjoy it."

Michael took a sip of his drink. "That's what I mean. There will always be war. We went to war over other things. Religion doesn't cause war. It's ways about thinking. If we all thought the same, there would still be a war, because then all of us would be doing the same and drive each other nuts."

Kax laughed. "When you put it that way I see your point. Hey, when Skyler comes back, do you want to mess with his head and say were engaged?"

"Most do. This is a world without faith, hope and it's sad. My planet, we don't believe in the same God, but we believe in something that's almost the same, and it's a nicer place to be." Michael smirked. "And if it involves tormenting Skyler, I'll do it."

Skyler strolled up to the table and took his seat. He had a big grin on his face. "So what did I miss?"

The waitress was still in the hallway fixing her top.

Kax batted her eyelashes at Michael. "Can I tell him?"

Michael grinned. "No, let me honey." Michael held Kax's hand.

Skyler's eyes were wide and he was shaking his head in confusion. "What's going on here?"

Michael's grin got bigger. "Kax and I are engaged."

Skyler's face went white. He tried to speak. "You what..." Everything went black in Skyler's mind and he fell out of the booth.

Michael and Kax couldn't stop laughing.

Kax noticed Skyler was not getting up. They both went to Skyler's side as the waitress came over.

Michael checked Skyler pulse and announced. "He's fine. He just fainted."

Everyone stopped worrying. Michael propped up Skyler in the booth against the wall.

Kax took a deep breath and calmed down. "Did you see Skyler's face when you said that. It was so funny. I think he believed you."

Michael got Skyler back into the both. "Finally, pay back."

The food soon arrived as Skyler was waking up. He saw the food, and the smell helped him open his eyes. "Is this real, did I really figure out how to time travel?"

Michael narrowed his eyes. "No, you didn't, we're in an old-fashioned restaurant."

Skyler became more awake. "Oh, you're right I almost forgot where I was."

Kax tried not to laugh at Skyler. "Almost?"

Skyler looked down at his food. "Mm that looks so great and the portion is enormous."

Michael took a bite of his food. "I wouldn't say that, I think they're big or large, not enormous."

"Yours looks gigantic compared to my tiny portion," Kax stated, pointing at her food.

Michael examined his food. "The size of all our portions seems to be quite off."

Skyler grinned. "I know why mine's the biggest."

Kax rolled her eyes. "Ya, because you're full of hot air and you need something to fill it up."

Michael tried not to choke on his food. "Good thing the food is bottomless, thanks to you know who, so you can order as much as you want."

"I think it is the style of my food is more appetizer style, not the main course."

"It's small and served in a sundae dish on a plate to put the stardust on when you're done," Michael pointed out.

Kax frowned. "What do you mean? You eat the star dust?"

"You suck on the crystal balls and then spit them out when the flavor is gone."

Kax shook her head. "No, you don't you let them sit they become soft in the sauce and eat them, watch me." She took her spoon and put a clear crystal stardust ball in her mouth covered in sauce and bit down on the stardust ball and crunched it up.

Michael's brow raised. "That's weird. I have to try one." He took his spoon and took a stardust off Kax's plate and tried to bite down. "Ow, that almost broke my tooth!" He spat the ball out onto his plate.

Skyler tried one. "Ow that almost broke my tooth too. How are you doing this?"

Kax shifted her eyes. "I don't know?"

Michael looked closely at Kax and noticed her teeth. "You have sharp teeth. I bet they could cut wires. Is that from being a Catillion?"

She felt her teeth with her tongue. "I have no idea. I guess so. I never paid attention to it. This is just how I was taught to eat it."

Michael gripped his head in pain. He let out a loud cry as the chandelier fell from above onto the floor next to their table, shattering into a thousand pieces. They jumped and Michael's head throbbed. "Dammit, sometimes I hate electricity. Why did that stupid Benjamin Franklin invent it!"

Skyler got up and brushed the glass off him. "You waited for us on Earth to discover electricity before you learned about your abilities?"

Michael cleaned himself off too, and the staff came running. Michael laughed. "No, we had something else with wires that was around before and turned out it worked well with your electrical system."

The manager came over to them. "I am sorry about this, your meal's on the house. Would you like us to seat you at a different table?"

They all shook their head at the tall male manager.

Skyler smiled. "It's okay, we weren't really hungry but if you need someone to fix it, my friend here is a Squallite and he likes fixing this kind of thing."

Michael sighed. "Yes, I am, and the broken wire is going to give me a headache. I can fix it if you want?"

The manager smiled. "Well, we don't like to put our customers to work, but how far do you have to be from the site to not have a headache?"

Michael regarded the three loose wires. "If you have a rubber cap, I can cap the wires until you get someone and that will stop it, but three loose ends that large; we're looking at 100 feet."

The manager nodded. "I can do that in a minute and I can reorder your food."

"Sounds good," Skyler said. "Thank you for being so kind to us."

The waitress guided them over to a table near the back.

Kax sighed. "I wish we would have just eaten that stupid spaghetti."

Skyler squeezed in next to her. "We had to get out of there, it was too stressful. I wish we could graduate right now and be having an adventure."

Michael frowned. "But we would have the stress of what to wear. I'm glad they now let you wear the dress uniform to the ceremony instead of those dumb gowns."

Skyler grinned. "I am not worried. I am going to graduate a captain."

"You can't graduate a captain!" Kax pointed out. "The highest rank you can graduate is lieutenant third class."

"I don't let rules get in my way. I'll figure something out." He smirked.

## Chapter 20

Back at the school, the exams were almost done for the week and they were all happy. It was so stressful that Kax's hair thinned out and Michael got a few white hairs. They weren't sure if Skyler did because of his blond curls; they couldn't tell if his would highlight or not.

Once the midterms were finished came the hard part. If they did well here, they needed to do well the rest of the year because that would determine if they advanced.

Skyler was in the courtyard sitting by the large stone fountain, waiting for the others to show up. He spotted Kax from a distance. He was going to get up and wave to her, but he saw she was with someone. A tall male brunette who kind of resembled Michael. Skyler thought it was him at first. So he stood up to look over at them more closely. He saw Kax and the man kiss. His heart pounded. He noticed the guy had a large nose, something Michael didn't have, and he seemed taller and slimmer. He noticed the guy's eyes and could clearly tell they were orange. He knew then she was with another Squallite. A sharp pain like an ice pick went through his chest. He wanted to pass out.

Michael showed up behind Skyler. "Hey, buddy, you ready for combat training?"

Skyler was frozen, watching Kax make out with the older Squallite.

Michael tapped him on the shoulder and he noticed what Skyler was watching.

Kax finished her goodbye with the guy and headed over to Michael and Skyler, who were trying to act as if they hadn't seen anything. She came over smiling. "Hey, guys, ready for practice?"

Skyler put on a phony smile, pretending he wasn't hurt by seeing Kax with another man. "You bet."

Throwing a few fake punches like a boxer, Kax laughed and peeled off her cadet uniform to reveal a black tank top. Skyler admired her body for a second.

Michael took off his shirt as well.

They were all wearing their colored pants and black tank tops.

They were ready and began sparring.

\*\*\*

Michael noticed a clear shot to knock Skyler to the ground.

Skyler fell backward, hands in the air, right into a group of passing older security cadets.

All three of them froze.

One of the guys' eyes filled with rage. "What do you think you're doing, pipsqueak?"

Skyler got up and stepped back. "Dude, I didn't mean to hit you. My friends and I were just sparring."

The gang of security cadets moved closer to Skyler. "Keep your paws off me, you stupid first year."

Michael stepped in. "It won't happen again. No reason for this to turn into something bigger. We're sorry and let's leave it alone."

The security cadet narrowed his eyes at Michael. "Fine, if you say so, we will leave you alone."

He smirked and stepped away.

Two of the other security cadets were starting to give Kax a hard time.

Rage instantly filled Skyler.

Kax tried to push the guys off her but couldn't.

Skyler punched one of the guys out.

The leader glared at Michael. "You said it wouldn't happen again and look what's going on. I should have known better than to trust an electric rat!"

Michael was insulted, but before he could take a swing at the leader, a guy on his right swooped at him. He blocked the guy, and the leader punched him in the stomach.

Kax was free thanks to Skyler's help. She joined in the fighting. There were five security cadets and only three of them. How could they win?

Michael was holding his own until they started to gang up on him.

Skyler was tiring of all this and he was getting stronger with frustration and rage. Finally, Skyler had a clear shot at the leader. He went for the swing when he felt someone grab his arm.

All the fighters looked up and saw four big admirals clustering around them. Skyler smirked. "Busted."

Everyone's eyes shifted to Skyler.

*** 

All the cadets were taken to Fleet Admiral Cane's office and waited to be summoned into the room. Fleet Admiral Cane called Michael, Skyler, and Kax in to see him first. He shook his head. "I know you three like to break rules and do your own thing, especially you, Skyler, but this is serious. The United Galactic Forces does not approve of public violence. Sparring is fine, but to cause harm to others is supposed to mean suspension. I do believe you are innocent. I have reviewed the security tapes. But that still doesn't excuse you. You leave me in a difficult spot. Do you have anything to say for yourselves?"

They all examined each other. "Sir, we meant no harm and are willing to take on whatever punishment you give to us," Michael said.

The fleet admiral shook his head. "See, now that's the problem. You three don't learn lessons, and you are obedient and willing to go the extra mile. But you need to learn not to get into trouble. I could kick you out, but you would find your way back in. I could send you to the front lines and you would survive and think it was a reward. There is nothing I can do to punish you."

They all sat there in silence.

"Here we go. I got something and I don't know if you will like it, but I am taking you out of your classes and sending you to the scrap yard."

Michael's eyes widened. "Please, sir, loose wires hurt my head."

The fleet admiral sighed. "I'm sorry, Michael, but with the recent attacks we need extra hands. If the wires hurt, go to the doctor and get something for it. But my decision is final. Your job will be to go through the scrap and find if there are any parts worth saving and you will divide the kinds of scrap up. You are excused from the rest of your exams and will start the job tomorrow. Until then I wish for you three to stay in your rooms."

They all agreed. Michael lifted his hand slightly. The fleet admiral saw and nodded slightly to let him know he could speak.

"Sir, if I may, can I please before we are sent to the rooms stop at the clinic to get something for my head."

"Yes, you may. I then want you three to stay out of trouble. I have to file a report and explain what happened every time one of you three breaks the rules."

They nodded in understanding. The fleet admiral took a deep breath. "All three of you can leave my office now."

They all got up and left together, heading out of the building.

Michael turned to his friends. "If you would like to follow me, you can, I guess. I'm going to the doctor."

Skyler smiled. "We will follow. You need someone to keep you company."

# Chapter 21

Dr. Kelley pulled up Michael's chart. "So, Mr. Jones, what can I do for you today?"

Michael sighed. "Well, Doctor, all three of us were sent for junkyard duty for the next two weeks. I asked not to because loose wires give me headaches."

Dr. Kelley studied Michael's chart. "Really, that's odd for a Squallite. Your race smells electricity and then their ears tingle for loose wires, but typically they don't get headaches. How long has this been going on?"

Michael paused. "All my life, and it stays until the wire is fixed. I have learned to work with the pain but not for long periods. That's why I am here; I need pain killers or something."

Dr. Kelley took out his stethoscope and listened to Michael breathe. He checked his blood pressure. Then checked his tablet one more time. "I can prescribe you something. I hope it will work. Since the Squallite race doesn't typically get headaches, there aren't many medications made for them out there, but let's try this one and see."

Michael sat there listening to Dr. Kelley. "Thank you, Doctor, and what should be done about Skyler?"

Michael got off the table. "I will keep an eye on him and thanks for the pills."

Dr. Kelley hit a few buttons on his tablet. "You can have the pills picked up at the pharmacy next door. They will be ready by the time you get there. I do recommend only taking two a day with meals. Let me know if anything changes."

Chapter 22

Morning came, and that meant the start of their extra duties. They all met up in the cafeteria for breakfast and headed off to the scrap yard. Michael's pills kicked in because his head only tingled around loose wires and didn't hurt.

A man in a gray officer's uniform came over to them. He checked his tablet. "I guess you three are the new kids. I am Officer Martins." The gray hair large-bellied scruffy officer handed them their gray jumpsuits. "Here are your uniforms. Put them over your cadet uniforms and return them at the end of the day."

He printed off a sheet of paper from his tablet. "Here is a list of all the scrap parts we are trying to locate and a picture of them next to the name; if you find them check it off and call it in on your phones, until then just sort them into piles." He handed them all a copy of the list. He printed off another sheet, then he handed them something resembling watches, but instead of a clock, there was a big green button and a light on the side.

He showed them how to use them and said, "If you come across a sheet of metal and you don't know what it is, hit the button and it will say what kind it is so you know where to place it." He checked his tablet, "That seems to be it, and if you need anything, call me but that is all. Go through those doors and pick an unsorted pile and start working."

They all headed off to the bathroom and started getting changed. Once they were done, they headed off to the scrap piles.

Skyler stared at the mountains of scrap ahead of him. "This is so gross, why do we have to do this?"

"Think about it this way. You want them to make new ships? Well, they have to recycle the old stuff. There are still lots of good working parts in here, but they need to be found." Michael patted Skyler on the back, "Your dad's ship is in this building somewhere."

Kax looked around. "Ya, but it's all dirty. It's something you never really think about."

Skyler's eyes bulged. "My dad's ship is in this junk pile?"

Michael shook his head. "Not in the junk piles but somewhere in this dome from what I remember."

Kax frowned. "Engineers wear blue. Why is Martins wearing gray?"

Michael tuned focus to Kax. "Because he will never go to space. He is a ground crew engineer; all ground crews, no matter their division, wear gray. Also he is human and not a Squallite. Most Squallites go to space so you will rarely see us wearing gray."

"Wait, why go through all the years of training then just to work in a junkyard?"

Michael shrugged. "I'm guessing with his rank and his age he took the job at year four and didn't go any higher. He hires people like us to sort the junk, so they can take the different metals, melt them down into other parts for new ships or weapons. Right now, we have the worst job in the entire forces."

Kax rolled her eyes. "Great, thanks a lot for telling me."

Michael shrugged. "Well, it's not my fault, and it can't be that bad. Come on let's go and get started on our work. Hey, where did Skyler go?"

Kax glanced over her shoulder. "I think he ran off while we were talking."

Michael saw a little blond and gray dot running in the distance. "He probably went to go look for his dad's ship. I'll go after him. He's going in the wrong direction. You start working."

Michael left Kax and ran after Skyler. Damn, for having short legs, he is so fast. Finally, Michael got caught up to him near the edge of the dome. He tackled him because Skyler was not stopping.

Skyler lay on the ground. "Ow! Dude why did you tackle me like that?"

"Because you were running and weren't stopping. You sure can run fast." Michael stood up and dusted himself off. "I told you I would show you where your dad's ship was and I will. It's not here, come with me and I will show you."

"I played lacrosse in high school." Skyler got up and looked around. "Where is Kax?"

"Working, where we should be. But this means something to you, so I will show you quickly and then we go back to work?" Michael held out his hand. "Deal?"

Skyler shook Michael's hand. "Deal."

Michael took Skyler though the paths in the junkyard. Finally, near the back of the dome, they saw old ships broken and beyond repair, some dating back to the beginning to the federation. They walked for a while until they got close to the end of the ships.

Skyler's eyes sparkled when he saw the black metallic dented up body. In large scratched out white letters read what was left of 'HMSS BLACKSTAR RSC-681.' "There it is!" He ran up the side of the ship and rubbed his hand along the side. It was the only black ship they had in the dome. It lacked one of its engines and many of the metal panels. Enormous cuts slashed the sides of the ship.

"Wow, this ship has seen better days." Michael stood and watched Skyler pet and hug the ship.

"It's still my dad's ship no matter how ripped up it is." He walked over to the door. "You coming or are you just going to stand there?"

"It's a condemned ship; you can't go in there. Do you know the unlock code?"

Skyler went over to the keypad to the door and typed in a few numbers. "520. It's my birthday, my dad used it for lots of things." The door opened and Skyler stepped in.

Michael went in after Skyler. "Okay, you got past the front door, but there is no power hooked up to this. The doors may not open anymore."

Skyler turned around and stared into Michael's eyes. "I asked you to come with me because you showed me the ship and you're a nice guy. I didn't say anything rude when your dad was dying. Just let me have this time with my dad."

He put his hand on Skyler's shoulder. "I am sorry, do what you need to do. Take your time. I will help in any way I can."

Skyler went ahead and opened the door to the rest of the ship. To his left was the door to the bridge and to the right was the hallway that took him to the rest of the ship.

Without hesitation, he veered to the right and went down the hall. He passed a few doors until he found one that had already been opened. He stood in the doorway and his eyes followed around the room. His heart pounded and his hands trembled. He saw a maroon room with metal paneling pulled from the walls and floor. The only furniture in the room was the built-in bed against the back wall and the desk.

He went over to the hardwood bed. There was no mattress or blankets, just the frame of the captain's bed. He laid down on the hardwood and watched the ceiling.

"I am guessing this was your dad's room?" Michael stepped into the room.

Skyler laid on his back and admired the ceiling. "Ya, this was where the magic happened. I was conceived in this bed. And my crib used to be right over there." He pointed behind him to the half wall that divided the old sitting area.

"That's probably the spot where he used to sleep with Kax's mother too."

Skyler frowned. "Oh right, ya, he probably had a bunch of women in this bed. Good memories."

"Good memories. This place has seen better days."

"You're right, but it is nice to be back here." He reflected on all the adventures his dad went on and all his conquests in and out of the bedroom. But no matter how hard of a day he had, his father always came back to his bed and was able to relax and start again.

Michael circled the room. "Not to be rude, but how much longer are you going to be?"

Skyler sat up in the captain's bed. "We can move on, there is one more place I've got to see." He got off the bed. Before he left the room, he glanced back at the room, took a deep breath. "I miss you, Dad."

He moved up the hall, back towards the bridge. This time he tried to open the door. He put his fingers between the doors and tried to slide them open. "Damn, it's no use. Michael can you get me in here?"

Michael examined the doors and how they were sealed. "No, I can't. They are sealed on purpose. Even if I had access, I think the doors are welded shut. The same person who opened your father's door is probably the one who welded this shut."

Skyler sighed and took a long pause. He whispered, "Cane." He cast a glance around the area. "Is there another way to get into the bridge?"

"There is one way; through the ventilation system. But I don't know if you can fit, it was only made for Squallites."

"Could you get in there and find a way to open the door from the inside?"

Michael paused. "I could try, but what is so important about the bridge? You want to sit in your dad's old chair and pretend you're captain or something?"

"My dad died in that room."

"Oh." He took a step back. "I will be right back."

Skyler put his hand on the door and wished he could just step right through those doors.

A few moments later, Skyler heard a 'clink and clank' above him, then a thunk.

"Can you hear me, Skyler?" Michael called though the door.

"Yes, I can. Can you open the doors?"

"I can, but I was right. They are welded shut from the inside. It's not pretty in here, but I think I can pull off the doors. This bridge is in pretty bad condition, pulling a few panels off the wall will be easy. Stand back and give me a few moments."

Skyler stepped back. All he heard was 'clink, clank and rattle and tear.' Finally, the doors moved and Skyler stepped onto the bridge.

His chest tightened, and a tear moistened his eye. The tops of the seats were burnt up. The lights on the ceiling and panels were falling down and loose. The walls had burn marks from the controls that had blown up. "Did you see this before you opened the door?"

Michael shook his head. "Not really, I just looked for the door. But, wow, this place really got heated before it crashed."

Skyler dropped his gaze to his feet and saw the blackened burned floor. "I've never heard the full story. My mother refuses to tell me and Cane told me the basics. I was only five." Tears came to his eyes.

Skyler only had a couple of years with his father and his bond was this strong. I wonder what will happen to me when my dad goes? My dad is all I have in the world.

Michael placed his hand on Skyler's shoulder. "We don't have to stay if you don't want to."

Skyler shook his head and went over to the captain's chair, which was in the middle of the room. He clamped his hand on the back of the chair. "When I was little, my dad used to let me sit in his chair and pretend to be captain. I was only on two missions with him after the one when I was born. But sometimes he would let me sit on his lap while he worked."

The tears poured down his face. He examined the blackened floor. There were two foot prints. "That must be where he was standing," He whispered. He placed his feet over the footprints and stood in the same spot, next to his father's chair. He took a deep breath, holding back as many tears as he could, trying to stay brave. He began to fall.

Michael rushed up behind him and helped him into the captain's chair. "Skyler, I think we should go."

Skyler covered his face wiping the tears. "He was standing there when he died. Why did he have to die? Why did he leave me?"

Michael put his hand on Skyler's shoulder. "Well, at least you had your mother."

"My mother's a bitch!" he snapped. "She didn't even want to tell me my father died. She said that he had to work late and refused to talk to me. Cane was the one who told me before I went to bed. He didn't know she didn't tell me."

"In her defense, you were five, but wow, that is harsh, I'm sorry about that. I can't imagine. My mother died in childbirth. My dad told me when I started asking questions."

"Cane tried to be there for me, but my mom got rid of him when I was twelve and she went and married Charles. I moved out when I was sixteen. I didn't even tell her I was joining the academy because I knew she would say no."

Michael patted Skyler on the back. "I'm sorry."

Skyler wiped the tears away from his face and stood up. "We've got to go. Can't sit around all day." He stood up and placed his foot over his dad's footprint one more time. "Hey, we're the same size." He took a deep breath and made his way out of the ship. Before he closed the ship door, he turned to Michael. "Thank you."

Chapter 23

The next day came, and it was back to junk yard duty. No more excuses; all three of them were working that day. They each took a different pile and started digging.

Skyler was having fun making lewd gestures with the scrap metal. Kax found them funny at the beginning. They managed to find a few parts on the list, but it wasn't easy.

She was tired, her hands hurt, and the sun was beaming down on her. She was so tired and not sure if she could go on. "Oh, my gosh, this is too hard. I'd rather be in a boring classroom all day. Why do you have to dig through all this crap? This sucks."

Michael yawned and wiped the sweat off his brow. "Thank you, Skyler, for giving us bad track records. I had no problems before you showed up."

Skyler pointed to a big clock. "It's not that bad, we've got about two more hours, then the day is done."

Kax threw a rock at Skyler. "Ya, two more hours today, but then we have to do it all again tomorrow. This is too much, we don't know how long we're here for, and it could be the rest of the year. We're missing valuable learning right now."

Michael sighed. "I really don't mind this, my classes are boring now. I have been ahead of them. I want the break. Falling behind would be the best way to get behind, and stay off the front lines."

"You know, we could try to get all of this junkyard cleaned up, then there wouldn't be anything else to worry about and they would have to give us better jobs."

Michael laughed at Skyler's idea. "We're not the only people working here. The forces have been trying to sort these piles for years. I bet if we dig deep enough we will find scrap from before our parents were born. Be happy this is a scrap pile and not a waste dump."

Kax wiped the sweat off her forehead with her wrist. "It's not the sorting I can't handle, it's the sun, it's so hot. I thought it was January, where is the snow?"

Michael gazed up at the top of the clear dome. "Well, you're going to hate this, Kax, but we're not outside. We are actually in a dome; a force field dome, so that when the sun is out, we will get the heat, but no snow or rain. It protects all this stuff from getting weather damaged. Not a bad idea, really."

Kax groaned. "Great, so we get the heat and a tan in the middle of winter."

"You know, a girl like you would look really good with a tan." Skyler winked.

Kax hurled another rock at Skyler. "Keep it up. I have an unlimited supply of rocks over here and, next time, I won't miss."

Michael laughed and went back to work. "You know, it wouldn't hurt to try to get all this stuff cleaned up."

Kax frowned. "I don't want to, but it might help, and maybe tomorrow will be colder."

Kax and the others were toiling away, trying to rush getting through these mountains of scrap. They tried to stay positive; every bit of scrap they cleared out, they got a little closer to finishing.

The hours rolled by slower and slower. The clock almost felt like it was stuck. Just before they were about to get too tired to work anymore, they heard the whistle blow. It was time to go home; work was done for the day.

All three of them went to the bathroom, changed their overalls and handed them in. They headed off; all tired and sore.

They made their way to the cafeteria and grabbed some dinner.

Kax sat with her food replicated steak. "This is going to suck, you know, doing the same horrible job every day."

Skyler poked at his food. "At least it keeps us out of trouble."

Michael picked at his food, too. "If they wanted me to stay out of trouble, then they should have separated me from you, that's where I need to be. Like I said, I was a perfect student until Skyler showed up."

Kax laughed. "That sounds about the same for me too. But I bet your life was boring, too."

"Sorry, buddy, about all this," Michael said. "It's not your fault."

Skyler smirked. "I know it's not my fault. Also by me breaking all these rules we have gotten lots of rewards too. How else would we be getting this extra experience?"

The gang looked at each other and nodded.

Michael ate some food. "I think we're all tired. We should just finish our food and head off to bed. It can't get any worse than this."


Chapter 24


The weeks passed and their jobs slowly got easier. They made a big dent by working so fast. It became more routine over time.

One morning, Michael woke up and rolled over in his bed to face Skyler's bed. "Skyler, I know this work was meant to teach us a lesson, but I think we should talk to the fleet admiral today. I am beginning to miss going to class."

Skyler rolled over and looked at Michael. "Sure, we can do that. I don't see a problem as we have been staying out of trouble."

Kax walked into the boy's room. She was all dressed and ready to go to work. "Come on, guys we're going to be late. I like it as much as you do, but we have to get going."

Michael sat up covering himself with blankets, "We're not going, we're going to go see Fleet Admiral Cane and tell him we're done and want to go back to classes."

Kax let out a big sigh of relief. "Hurray, I was wondering when we were going to do that. I'm sick of junkyard duty."

Skyler got out of his bed, exposing himself. He plucked the comb out of his nightstand and brushed the sleep curls out of his hair. With his back turned to Kax, he wiggled his butt at her. "You like what you see?" Skyler turned back and grinned at Kax.

She had covered her eyes.

Michael took the textbook off the table and smacked Skyler on the butt. "Put some pants on."

Skyler swung around and saw a disgruntled Michael behind him. His smile faded. He gathered his clothes off the floor and got dressed at the same time as Michael.

Kax kept her back turned from the guys.

Once they were dressed, it was straight to the fleet admiral's office. They were not going to do one more day of junkyard duty. When they got to the office, Fleet Admiral Cane's secretary stood up and blocked the door to the admiral. "What are you three doing out here? The admiral is not seeing anyone today. Please leave."

Skyler frowned. "I'm certain he will make the exception for me, I'm Skyler Therris."

She shook her head. "I'm sorry, Mr. Therris, but no one, and that means no one, is allowed to go past the door. The admiral wants to be alone."

Skyler narrowed his eyes. "Cane told me himself I am the exception to that rule. If I need to see him, I can at any time."

The secretary frowned. "Don't you dare come any closer or I will call security!"

Skyler didn't listen and went between her head and arm. He knocked on door and called out, "Cane! Its Skyler we need to talk!"

The secretary pushed Skyler away. "I told you to get out of here!"

Fleet Admiral Cane opened his office door. "You can let Skyler in, I need to talk to him."

The secretary moved from the door and let Skyler in and pointed at the other two. "You two, stay here."

Kax and Michael sat down in the waiting area.

***

Fleet Admiral Cane's hair was messy and his eyes were red, like he didn't get any sleep and had been crying.

"Are you alright, Admiral?" Skyler asked, sitting down on a chair.

Cane took a deep breath and sighed. "Skyler, did you tell your mother you were joining the United Galactic Forces?"

Skyler shook his head. "No, sir. I haven't talked to my mother in years."

Cane rubbed his face. "That's sad to hear. Because your mother called me last night."

Skyler put his head down and sunk into his chair. "Oh, I didn't know. I am very sorry, sir."

Cane shook his head. "She told me she called you a few weeks ago, too, and you didn't want to talk to her. What is going on, Skyler?"

Skyler shook his head. "Admiral Cane..."

The fleet admiral cut him off. "This is off the record, so call me Leon."

Skyler scratched his head. "Ok, um, Leon, my mother and I haven't really talked since I moved out when I was sixteen. She was away. I got into a fight with my step-dad and she never made much of an effort to contact me after that."

Leon sighed. "I see. Well, she was near retirement here, and thanks to her finding out about you here, she won't retire and wants you to quit."

Skyler frowned. "I'm not quitting. I know she never wanted me involved, but this is my dream. This is what I want to be doing. I won't quit for her or anyone."

"You remind me of your father when you talk like that."

Leon got out of his chair and went to the top drawer of his filing cabinet. He pulled out a bottle of sherry and two glasses. He poured one for Skyler. He took a drink. "I miss how your mother used to be before you were born."

Skyler took a sip. "Ya, I remember my dad mentioning it to me a few times; how she used to be and why he fell in love with her. But when I see her, I have no idea how she could be the same person."

"That sounds right, and I didn't know you still remembered your father."

Skyler put down his glass. "I don't remember much, but the memories I have of him, I wish to keep as long as I can."

Leon drank some more. "I'm glad you want to stay in United Galactic Forces. From what I have seen, you will be a great captain one day."

Skyler smiled and drank some more. "Thank you. So if my mom is still in, is she still a commodore or did she make admiral? And why haven't I seen her around?"

Leon drank. "She's still a commodore, and she doesn't teach. She is working for the switch boards. Also she is in Fleet Admiral Thomson's Fleet. Your father and I used to be in his fleet. Thompson might outrank me in years, but he doesn't outrank me in knowledge."

Skyler laughed and finished off his glass.

Leon poured him another one. "So I take it you don't like this step-dad?"

Skyler drank and shook his head. "Nope, and I don't plan to like him. Charles is an ass who never liked me. He kicked me out when I was sixteen and I went to live with my uncle."

Leon took a big sip finishing his glass. "Really, that bad. Damn him. I didn't know you were still there. You remember the one year I met you at your uncle's. I thought it was temporary. I only met your stepfather a handful of times and he was never nice to me."

Skyler drank some more. "He has never been nice, dumb government ass. It was temporary just until I joined the forces."

"You know your mother was the puzzle I could never figure out, but your dad did. I wish your dad was around to see how much of a fine man you have grown up to be."

Skyler scoffed. "I'm not that great, I've got my faults."

Cane laughed. "All men do, you'll grow out of it when you meet the right woman. Don't go getting married to your ship. That's a huge mistake many men make."

"No marrying my ship. Got it."

Leon smiled. "Thanks for cheering me up. Please call your mother and talk to her."

Skyler sighed. "Only if you take my friends and me off junk yard duty and put us back in the classroom."

Leon typed in a few things on his computer. "I will do that for you. Enjoy your day. You start classes Monday since the day's almost half over and it's Friday."

Skyler got up. "Sounds good to me. Thanks, Leon."

He went to open the door when Fleet Admiral Cane spoke up. "Oh, one more thing." He reached into his drawer and pulled out a box, got up and gave it to Skyler. "Your father gave this to me when I started as his lieutenant. It was so I never lost my way."

Skyler opened it to reveal an antique compass on a chain. He looked up at the fleet admiral. "Thank you so much, sir. This means a lot to me. I will treasure this with all my heart."

Cane patted Skyler's shoulder. "I am very glad to hear that. Now run along."

Skyler put the box in his pocket and exited the office. He saw his friends were falling asleep in their armless hover chairs. He approached them. "Well, we're off junkyard duty and we start classes Monday. We have the rest of the day off. How is that for negotiations?"

Michael stood up and hugged Skyler. "Thanks, but since when does a meeting with the fleet admiral involve alcohol?"

Skyler laughed and patted Michael on the back. "No negotiation is complete without drinking, don't you know that? Now come on, let's get loaded." He walked out ahead of them.

Michael and Kax followed Skyler out of the room to wherever he thought he was going.

## Chapter 25

A few drinks in, the joy faded from Skyler's face and he began to sulk. With a beer in this hand, he placed his head on the table at the bar he and his friends had visited.

"Skyler, what's wrong? You normally love bar time?" Kax asked.

Skyler slowly picked up his head. "I know but just too much is going on lately. I thought this would help relax me but it's not."

Michael took a sip of his drink. "Skyler maybe it is best you go back to the dorm and get some rest."

Skyler gave Kax a light smile. "Want to come be my roommate tonight?"

Kax took Skyler's beer away from him. "Time for you to go to bed. You need to rest, not have sex."

"We don't have to have sex. We could just cuddle?"

She shook her head. "Skyler I don't know what's the matter with you, but my answer is no. Now come on, you need some rest." She slid out of the booth and held out her hand.

He took her hand and got out of the booth.

Michael paid the bill and followed them back to the room.

\*\*\*

Late into the night, Michael woke up to the sound of someone's voice. As he woke up a bit more, he could recognize the voice to be Skyler's. He looked around quickly; the lights were off and Skyler was talking quietly. He listened and pretended to be asleep.

Skyler was on his phone. "Listen, I called so does it really matter what time I talk to you?" He sighed out of frustration. "Fine, I won't call you this late again. But I am not quitting. No, I will not tell you my dorm number. You won't listen to me! This is what I want to do. You never cared about me before, why are you starting to now?"

He shook his head. "That's it. Fine, be that way, but don't expect to hear from me again!" Skyler hung up his phone and threw it across the room. He went to his desk drawer and pulled out some hard liquor, drinking from the bottle. He took a deep breath, like he was going to cry, but didn't.

Michael could tell he was hurting on the inside. He wanted to say something to comfort his friend but couldn't. His friend would know he listened in on what he wanted to be a private time. Michael felt bad for him, and wished that he could help him, but there was nothing he could do but let Skyler be alone with his thoughts.

Skyler finished his drink, put the rest away and went back to sleep.

## Chapter 26

Getting back into the routine of going to class was harder than it seemed. There was so much that they had missed in the past couple of weeks and they wanted to get back on top.

During class Kax couldn't help but wonder about Skyler. He is cute, but he is so mysterious. He rarely talks about himself. I wonder what he is hiding?

After class, they all met up at the cafeteria. They got their food and were sitting there, eating shepherd's pie. Skyler picked at his food. "Dude, what do you think the food replicator uses to make potatoes out of?"

Michael stared at his food. "Same thing they use to make all the food out of, it changes the taste."

Kax frowned. "I don't like the food replicator, it's not right. How are we to get our vitamins from things that are not real?"

Michael smiled sarcastically. "Well, if they just put in vitamins, it would all end up tasting the same."

Skyler frowned. "Do we have to always have the same conversation here? We all know the food sucks here, it's not real, and it's never going to be, so can we all stop arguing about it?"

Michael and Kax stared at Skyler. "Sorry, buddy, I didn't know it bothered you so much," Michael replied. "You're the one who started it though."

Skyler shrugged. "Ya, sure, you're right. Don't worry about me, go back to saying whatever. I don't care."

Kax frowned at Skyler. "You know you have been acting a bit odd lately. Care to share?"

She hoped she had picked the right time to ask Skyler all the questions she had wanted to know.

Skyler continued the shrug. "Nothing, really. I'm starting to feel bad, I have dragged you all into my mess. Because I'm a punk, as you would say."

Michael frowned. "That's it, nothing else? We're your friends, and it's fine. You haven't done anything wrong. We like you. If we didn't care for you, we would have stopped hanging out with you a long time ago."

Kax nodded. "He's right. If we didn't like you, we would have blamed you and never talked to you again."

Skyler looked up from his food and smiled. "So, you both think of me as a friend?"

Michael groaned. "Well, a friend you love to hate."

Kax nudged Michael. "Yes, Skyler, we do."

Skyler laughed. "That is great. I'm happy you are my friends. So now that we're official friends, how about we all ask each other one question about ourselves and be truthful about the answers."

Kax smiled. This was what she had been waiting for, the moment where they could ask Skyler anything and get the answers about who he was and he would have to be honest.

Michael went to say something but Skyler stopped him and asked Kax, "So what do you think of me? Do you like me in any way or am I wasting my time?"

Kax rolled her eyes. She knew it, he wasn't here for anything else. Great, this is just another excuse to hit on me. She smiled politely. "Maybe if you weren't a playboy and a jerk most of the time, there would be a chance, but no, you kill it every time. I only like you as friend." We're supposed to be honest. She released a deep breath. "You are cute."

Skyler grinned, as if his ego had gone up ten points. "I understand. So any questions you want to ask me?"

This is it. She smiled smugly. "Okay, then my question. Where do you get all your money?"

Michael did a double take at Kax's question.

"My uncle, before I joined, gave me a large amount of money, that's all."

"So your family is rich?"

Skyler waved his finger. "Ah, you are only allowed to ask one question." He faced Michael. "So it's your turn. What do you want to ask me?"

Michael paused contemplating his question. "Is your family rich?"

Skyler smiled and shook his head. "Not really, my uncle is. He is loaded, my mother invested her money well, and we have more money than most, but we're not living in the lap of luxury. And my step-dad has a well-paying job as governor. I am not rich, I've got no source of renewable income. My money was given to me by my uncle when I graduated. When it is gone, I will have nothing."

"I see, makes sense. So now, Skyler, what question are you going to ask me?"

Skyler paused for a moment in deep thought. "Nothing. I'll ask you your question later, when it's the right time."

"Hey, that's not fair," Michael objected.

Skyler grinned. "I didn't say when we had to ask the questions."

Kax rolled her eyes. *Just when I thought he could change.*

Skyler got up. "Come on, guys, let's get out of here and get real food."

Kax didn't feel like getting up. She sat there staring at him.

He looked down at her and gave her puppy dog eyes. "Come on, first week back was hard, but now it is the weekend. Let's go out and have some fun!"

*Dammit, I can't resist those sad green eyes. He is cute, I just wish I knew if I could trust him.* She smiled and rose out of her seat. "I guess you're right, let's have some fun."

Michael also got up. "Well, if you two are going."

Skyler smirked. "This is great. Come on, we can get some real food and go shopping I need some new pants."

How many pairs of pants does this guy need? Kax paused. "Sounds great, let's get going and have some fun."

All three of them headed to the garage and got on the bike. They made their way to the city with high hopes for a fun time.

Chapter 27

They drove around on the little bike hunting for a place to hang out. As they were driving, Skyler saw the mall. He called out. "Hey guys lets go to the mall!"

Michael changed lanes and headed to the mall. He went to the parking garage where he pulled in. They hit a few buttons on the wall of the garage and it instantly teleported them and their bike to a parking spot in the garage. From there, they all walked down to the attached garage. Once in, a Mall-Bot greeted them. The Mall-Bot looked like the torso of a human male, all in metal, levitating above the floor. The Mall-Bot spoke in a deep masculine electronic voice.

"Hello, and welcome to the mall. How may I direct you to where you would like to go?"

Skyler spoke to the Mall-Bot. "We just want to walk around the mall and window shop."

The Mall-Bot replied with. "If you wish to walk around the outside of the mall, the doors are to your left. Once you are done, you can make your way to level three. Here you will find the home improvement store."

There was a light from the Mall-Bot's chest and a map of the mall showed up with a path depicting how they could get to the home improvement store. The Mall-Bot gave them a minute to view the map. "Would you like me to guide you there?"

"No, we just want to explore the mall." Skyler spoke in a disgruntled tone.

The Mall-Bot promptly replied, "Outdoor Explorer, that store is located on level two, would you like me to take you there?" The map changed to show the store.

He clenched his fists. "Food court. We're going to the food court."

The Mall-Bot turned off the light "Our food court has over 100 restaurants and five-star dining. From fast food to import, we have it all. The..."

Skyler yelled at the Mall-Bot. "Shut up. I don't care. And do not follow us!"

The Mall-Bot stated, "Please enjoy your stay at the mall. Would you like to rate my service on a scale of 1-10 on how helpful I was? Ten being least and one being best."

Skyler's face was red. "100! You were horrible!"

"That is not a valid answer. Please select, from 1-10, how helpful I was with 10 being least and one being best."

He was about to punch the Mall-Bot when Michael restrained him. "Come on, let's get going, we don't need to destroy a useless Mall-Bot." Michael dragged Skyler away.

As they strolled around the mall, they noticed other people walking with their Mall-Bots. They saw two types of distinct Mall-Bots. One model appeared more masculine with a boxed shape and rectangle head. The other model appeared more feminine with a curved body and oval head. But both had no lower legs and hovered, and had square LED screens in the middle of their chests.

"So, Skyler, where do you want to go?" Michael asked.

Skyler grumbled. "I don't know where you buy pants."

"At a store, where else? There are lots of clothing stores here."

Skyler glared. "I really have never been in this mall before. I'm not used to this one." He stopped walking and spun in a circle taking in all the surrounding stores. They continued ahead until Michael spoke up. "There's a store called Hot Studs. I think that might be what you're looking for, Sky."

Skyler sharply pivoted around and glared at Michael. "Where did you get that map? And don't call me Sky, that's a girl's name, and I hate it."

Michael handed Skyler the list of stores and answered, "Sorry, I thought I would give you a nickname. And when you weren't looking, I asked a Mall-Bot for a print out of the mall directory."

Skyler frowned. "If you call me Sky again, I will start calling you buggy boy, and don't ever talk to another Mall-Bot. I hate them."

Michael scoffed. "You could have fooled me."

Kax tossed her hair and flashed Skyler a smile. "What would you do to me if I started calling you Sky?"

"Sweet cheeks, hot ass or sexy, whatever one bothered you most coming from me."

Her smile faded. "Fine, you win. No more Sky."

They kept on walking and headed down to the store Michael had pointed out. The walls of the store were painted black and lights were flashing while electro music played.

Skyler was grinning away. This was his kind of store. Skyler entered and felt like he was in a night club with clothes displayed on the walls.

Kax was feeling intimidated. She asked Skyler. "Why would you buy clothes in a store that looks like a night club?"

Skyler couldn't stop grinning. "Because then you can see how the clothes will look on you in a night club environment, which is where you will be wearing them."

"Do they have a women's section at least?" Kax asked.

Michael pointed to the corner with the tight leather pants and sparkly tops. "I think that's what you're looking for Kax."

Kax raised an eyebrow and made her way over to the display.

Skyler started inspecting a pair of shiny leather pants when a blue-skinned salesman came up to him and Michael. "Is there anything I can help you gentlemen find?"

"I'm looking for something different. I have a few pairs of leather pants but they're plain, and I want something that says, 'Wow look at him.' Do you know what I mean?"

"I think I know what you're looking for." The salesman smiled at Michael. "You okay with me selling your boyfriend some super sexy pants?"

Michael laughed. "He's my roommate, not my boyfriend."

The salesman winked at Michael. "Whatever you say, do you want me to find you something as well?"

He shook his head. "No, that's okay, I'm good."

He looked Michael over. "You're too cute to walk around wearing those clothes, you could do so much more. Come on, you're getting something that everyone will be jealous of."

He strutted off. Michael and Skyler followed him.

\*\*\*

Kax was examining a bunch of glitter tank tops. She didn't know which one would look better on her. A saleslady came over to her. "Hey, there, wondering what that will look like on you?"

"I have a few shirts, but just trying to see if there is anything that will make me pop. Do you know what I mean?"

The human saleslady smiled. "Take the tops you want and come with me."

Kax followed the lady to the mirror, and she took the top and held it in front of Kax. In the mirror, the top appeared to be on Kax, as if she was wearing it. Kax gaped. She looked at her chest to see the top was not on her, but in the full-length mirror it appeared that she was wearing it. "Wow, that is great, it looks like I'm really wearing the top."

The saleslady smiled. "I am glad you like it. This one is a new feature the malls are just starting to get. It takes the image of you from what is sees and simulates what the outfit will look like on you. It works in different sizes too." She then took a larger size of the same top and showed Kax the difference.

Kax was all giddy. "Oh, my. I love this. I want them all now."

She passed Kax a purple top. "If you want to impress that guy you came in with I recommend this one."

Kax blushed and pointed to Skyler. "Oh, I already have his attention."

"Not that one. The tall one, I think I heard his name was Michael?"

"Oh ya, he's cute too."

The saleslady laughed. "I will leave you be and you can go and pick out all your clothes. The checkout is right over there."

***

Skyler was trying out the pants the salesman showed him in the mirror, but Skyler wanted to see how they would feel if he wore them, not just the way they looked. He tried on a few; some were too tight, some were too dull. He was getting frustrated. He wanted something that would make him pop and have the women want him more than they already did.

The salesman came over to him with one more pair of pants. He handed them to Skyler. "These are not normal pants, they are

Fiendnix skin and are specially imported. They even have their own dial that comes with them. These are one of a kind pants. What you do is, you place them on and turn the dial from a sparkle shine to glow or dull."

Michael frowned. "Isn't the Fiendnix the Cassiopeians' most sacred animal? How did someone kill one and bring it to Earth?"

The salesman shrugged. "I don't know, I just sell the products."

Michael glared at Skyler. "I would worry about those pants. Even if you can have them on Earth, but you might offend a Cassiopeian."

Skyler smirked. "In that case, I'll take them, doesn't matter to me. We're going to war with them why can't I offend them."

Michael wrinkled his mouth. "If you say so, Skyler, I just think this is a bad idea."

Skyler glanced over at Michael. "You getting anything? I know you tried on a few things."

Michael shook his head. "Not really, I was only looking because you were."

Skyler patted Michael on the back. "Nonsense, you pick up what you want and I will put it on my bill."

Michael went to the back and picked up a pair of pants and a jacket.

Kax came over to Michael, holding a few tops and a pair of pants.

"Michael, you would look great in a pair of leather pants. Especially with your long legs." She winked.

Michael shrugged. "I guess I never really thought about it like that. They were always too expensive for me to consider a pair."

She laughed. "They are, but next to the type of pants Skyler is buying the moon looks cheap."

Crash! A loud crash thundered as they made their way out of the store. The store gates closed, sirens wailed and red flashing lights started spinning. "Lock down. Lock down, there is an attack on the building. All mall customers are asked to go to the nearest exit and wait. Stay with a security team member!"

Skyler scanned around them. "Where is this attack? I don't see anything?"

"Could it be a drill?" Kax asked.

There was another loud crash, this one right in front of them. An almond shaped spacecraft tore right through the ceiling. A line of mall-bots rushed towards the craft. The ship landed and a group of well-armed Cassiopeians came out shooting.

Michael grabbed Kax and Skyler and pulled them behind a wall.

The Cassiopeians shot at the mall-bots, blasting them to pieces.

"Alright, take that, mall-bots!" Skyler cheered, his joking words a contrast to his tense face.

Michael covered his mouth. "Stop that, they will hear us."

Kax tapped both their shoulders. "Um, guys. . ."

A group of four Cassiopeians stood with guns right in front of them.

Skyler snatched the fire extinguisher and bashed one on the head with it, knocking him into another one. He picked up their guns and handed one to Michael.

"Kax, stand behind me!" Skyler said.

Skyler and Michael aimed their guns at the two remaining Cassiopeians.

The Cassiopeians let down their weapons. One of them spoke with a hiss. "Talls one, are yous a Ssquallite?"

Michael brushed his hair behind his ear. "I am, and these are my friends."

"Theys do nots keep you as Sslave?"

Michael shook his head. "They are my friends, and I'm here out of my own free will."

The Cassiopeian's consulted with the others. "Then yous three Sshall be spared. Sstay outs of the way of the bloodsshed."

Michael stood up. "No! There will not be any bloodshed! Leave this mall alone. I am not the only Squallite here, there are many others working in the walls of this mall. If you are worried about hurting Squallites, then attacking here you will hurt more. I suggest you leave!"

The lead Cassiopeian stared Michael dead in the eyes. "I haves my orders to destroys humanss in this place. Humanss must pays!"

Skyler spoke up. "Humans? Where do you see humans? Look around you at the people you are attacking, there are not many humans. Humanoid, but not human. You will hurt too many innocents. If your beef is with humans than go somewhere else!"

The lead Cassiopeian raised his arm and shot his gun at Skyler.

Kax pushed Skyler out of the way, just in time. The laser grazed the top of her left arm. She grabbed her arm and held it close.

Skyler fell to the ground.

Michael aimed his gun at the leader. "Get out or I will blow your heads off! You may not be able to hurt a Squallite but I am willing to hurt you!"

He fired two shots towards them purposely not trying to hit them.

They stepped back. The leader spoke. "You win this round but we will be back." The retreated to their ship.

Skyler stood up and dusted himself off. "What was that all about?"

"I don't really understand it, but Squallites helped the Cassiopeians a long time ago, and they have promised not to hurt us."

Skyler checked over Kax. "How's your arm?"

She removed her hand and showed him the burn mark. "It hurts, but it is just a simple burn."

Michael came over and examined it. "You barely got hit. You should be fine. Come on lets head home."

Chapter 28

When they got back to the room, Skyler relieved tension by playing with his new pants. The store had placed them in a box with instructions on how to care for them. He looked over at Michael. "Hey, how hard would it be to go and find a trailer for your bike so we can carry more?"

Michael picked his outfit out of the closet. "Never thought about it, but I can call a few people and see what I can find out. It will be pricy and rare."

Skyler nodded. "Since we don't have a car and all three of us have been using the bike, it would make sense to get one. And don't worry about the price. I'll cover it."

Michael thought about it. "Let's just try to find the part then talk about a deal. It might cost less than we're all expecting."

He read the instructions for his pants. "The instructions say I have a lifetime warranty, I plan to use these for as long as I'm single."

Michael laughed. "Then I guess you're never getting married?"

Skyler shook his head. "No plans to. But never say never."

Kax rolled her eyes. "Well, then, stud. When do you plan to go out and use these pants?"

Skyler answered, "I am not quite sure. I really want to wear them, but you can't wear these to any kind of bar. You've got to wear them somewhere special."

Kax read the instructions. "According to this, there is a regular mode. You can wear them everywhere."

Skyler took the instructions back from Kax and read them. "Ya, but I can't do that the first time out, you got to break this baby in at a really nice club. Let us celebrate at Diamandis for our victory of the attack at the mall."

They got to the club and there was a line in the front to get in. This annoyed Skyler. "That's not fair, why is there a line? I need to get some action now."

Kax laughed. "There are ten people in front of us, it's not a big line at all. Give us a few minutes and we will be inside."

Michael looked up. "You can hear the music from out here and there's plenty of people in the line. Why do we even need to go in?"

Skyler frowned. "What do you mean? We're not in there, where it is warm, there are drinks and more hot girls. You can't have the same fun out here."

Michael shrugged. "Ok, I guess, but really this is my first time at a club. Never been to one before."

Skyler gasped and grabbed his heart. "Are you serious? That is terrible, please, please tell me that's so not true."

Michael laughed and shook his head. "It's true, and it's no big deal."

Skyler tugged on Michael's arm and steered him to the front of the line. Kax followed them. Skyler went right up to the bouncer. "Sir, I know we cut the line, but this is an emergency. This man, my friend, just told me he had never been to a night club before, you have to let us in."

The bouncer glared at them. "Is that true? Spin around and tell me how much is the standard cover charge?"

Michael paused. He tried to use his local knowledge but really had no clue. "Cover charge? I've got money but how much is it?"

The bouncer laughed and unhooked the velvet rope. "You three can go in. I will waive the cover for the newbie, but you and the girl ten each."

Skyler paid for both, and they all walked in.

Michael stepped in and was overwhelmed by the lights, the noise and all the people. He stood there stunned not sure what he should do.

Skyler put his arm on Michael's shoulder and smiled. "Don't stand there like a bump on the log. Get out there, find a girl, and tell the bartender I sent you. He will give you the key to a room."

Michael was frozen. Skyler pushed him into the crowd and watched until his friend disappeared. He turned to Kax who was standing behind him. He grinned. "You want to dance."

Kax smiled. "Not with you, I prefer someone new."

Skyler grinned and inched closer. "Ok, then. My name's Jim. Want to dance?" He extended his hand.

Kax laughed and giggled. "Jim? That's your best? Okay, well, then. I'm Anita and I need a drink without you, Jim."

He frowned, upset that it didn't work.

Kax headed off to the bar.

Skyler made his way to the dance floor to show off his new pants. He danced for a few minutes, and then someone caught his eye. A long black-haired girl from across the floor, dancing and shaking her body like she didn't care.

She was a larger build, but still showed off her hour-glass figure. He watched her dance and move in her small tight t-shirt and her matching black mini skirt. He was frozen on the dance floor. He knew then that she was going to be his. He unfroze and pushed his way to the other side of the dance floor to get to her. Once he made it, he came up from behind her and tapped her on the shoulder. "Hey, good looking, care for a drink?"

She shot him a smile. She was taller than he was, but she didn't seem to mind. She and Skyler headed over to the bar. He ordered two drinks, one for her and one for him. They sat down at the bar and Skyler spun in his stool. He noticed from across the bar Kax was getting off her stool and leaving with an unfamiliar man. A pain shot through his chest and he let out a long sigh. He turned back around and looked at his girl. "So you come here often?"

She tossed her hair. "Maybe. How often do you?"

He grinned. "Not so much lately, but I have been here before." Skyler shifted in his seat, "So I take it you know this place has rooms upstairs?"

She sucked on the cherry in her drink. "I would love to try out one of the rooms with you." She leaned closer and stroked her fingers up and down his chest.

Skyler blushed and turned to the bartender. "Hey, barkeep, can I pay for the drinks and a key to one of the rooms?"

The bartender took off a set of keys from a hook on the wall. "Here you go. How will you be paying?"

Skyler pulled a hundred out of his wallet. "Cash, and keep the change."

They headed up to the room for some alone time.

\*\*\*

On the dance floor, Michael was having fun dancing, the one thing he finally felt he was good at. He didn't like the crowd pushing him because it was so tight and cramped. Finally, the sound changed, and a big circle in the floor opened up and one by one people went in and started dancing. He liked this idea, and waited for one dancer to go, and then another before he jumped in. He danced with only new moves. It was time to show off all the years of dancing alone to the world. They cheered him on. He didn't want to stop. He was glad Skyler had dragged him here.

As he danced on the floor as the center of attention all the problems in the world seemed to fade, it was a wondrous feeling of nirvana. He never wanted it to end. But like all great things, it had to.

He was dancing with his head back. When he brought it forward, he saw Kax in the distance. She was heading for the door and seemed to be crying. He stopped dancing and ran to see Kax. He got out the door and saw the strawberry blonde who had her hands in her face crying. He put his hand on her shoulder. "Hey, Kax, what happened?"

The girl turned around and frowned at Michael. "Who do you think you are touching me?"

Michael could see right away that he had made a mistake. He let go of her and raised his hands. "Sorry, I thought you were my friend, but I was wrong. She is also a Catillion."

She frowned again. "What are you trying to say, all Catillion look the same? And that's rude to call your friend Cat."

He laughed and shook his head. "No, her name is Kax. K-A-X, not Cat, and you aren't the same, just your hair color is, and from a distance I thought you were her. I'm sorry."

She frowned at him and answered him. "So I see. I guess thanks for coming out but you can go back in and deal with your own thing. I don't need you."

He shook his head. "I want to make sure you're okay first. Is there anything I can help you with?"

She shook her head and started to cry. "No, just leave me alone and go back to your friend."

He knew she was upset and something had happened. He didn't want to leave her side, no matter what she said. He stood there as she continued to cry.

"My boyfriend dumped me and he cheated right in front of me. He is such a jerk and here I thought he could be the one."

Michael held out his arm, offering her a sleeve to cry on. "Hey, don't you worry. It wasn't meant to be. You're an attractive girl. You can find someone else."

She frowned at him. "Oh, I can do better, but you're not interested in me? That's not encouraging. How am I supposed to believe you that I'm pretty if you're not interested?"

Michael took his hand off her shoulder and rubbed his chin. "I'm asexual. I don't know. I thought that's what you're supposed to say."

"You just made things worse." She threw her hands up in the air and stormed away.

Michael stood there confused.

Kax came up behind him and laughed. "You are too funny."

Michael whirled around and faced Kax.

She shook her head. "You're terrible with women. You could have just told her the truth that your gay and not lie about being asexual. She's never going to see you again."

Michael narrowed his eyes. "Who told you I was gay? Did Skyler tell you that? I'm straight for the record. I'm straight I'm just reserved."

Kax shook her head. "No there is just a rumor going around. But your secret is safe with me. I just don't know why you would lie like that?"

Michael looked Kax in the eyes and sighed. "For the record she wasn't my type. But it is a long story."

Kax stretched up, wrapped her arms around Michael. "I'm willing to listen."

He put his arms around her and hugged her. "You're a good friend. Let's find a place to sit down and I will explain everything."

Chapter 29

May came sooner than they had all thought. It was the month before their final exams and they were worried. They all met at the bar after classes to relax.

Skyler was on his second beer before the rest of them had finished their first.

Kax stared at Skyler's empty glasses. "Damn it. I wish we could take the exams now. Why are they making us wait? It's horrible. I hate exam preps. They're annoying."

Michael nodded. "You're right, I mean, sure. There is the studying we need to do, but why? It sucks. Wish I could just wake up and the exams would be all over."

Skyler sighed. "Well, the good news is my pants are awesome."

Kax glared at Skyler. "You're worried about pants that have their own insurance policy, but not the exams that determine if you get held back or keep going?"

Skyler grinned. "I've got it all figured out is all. I'm not worried about it one bit. Why worry? I'll be a captain one day."

Kax rolled her eyes. "Being held back will hold you back from being a captain and, if you are held back next year, you could get held back again. Then you're stuck."

Skyler shrugged. "I'll figure it out. My exams won't kill me. Yours might."

Kax cringed and drank her beer, "Damn, you had to remind me of that."

Michael snapped at Skyler. "You can be an asshole sometimes, you know that?"

Skyler sighed. "Listen, I'm sorry, the exams are bothering me too, okay, is that what you want to hear? I just am trying to put on a brave face, okay, guys?"

Kax studied her drink. I wish I didn't have to take my exams. If I take them, I could die. I know the stuff but what if I screw up?

Michael looked over at Kax. "Hey, don't worry, I'm sure you will be fine." He rubbed her shoulder. "My dad's not doing well. He is recovering a lot slower than expected. I hope me acing my exams will cheer him up, but I don't want to do too well because then I am closer to going to the front lines in this upcoming war."

Skyler gazed into his beer, worried. "Come on, cheer up everyone. Let's make a toast to our best year at the academy we ever had!"

Michael picked up his head and laughed. "What are you talking about? You're the only one who has been here for the year. Kax and I have already finished a few years."

Skyler laughed. "Ya, but did you have this much fun? I haven't heard any stories about your past roommates."

"I think you're right. At least it is the most eventful."

Skyler arched a brow at Kax. "And what about you, how was your last year?"

Kax shook her head. "I think you're right, this is one of the most fun years of my life."

Skyler grinned and lifted up his beer. "Then let's toast to the next year and the year after being better and better."

## Chapter 30

Skyler pulled out the manual and tossed it to Michael. "It says that the skin changed color and when the Fiendnix is skinned, it still has the ability to change colors and so they line it with a pad that has something in it that controls the coloring of the pants with the remote. It's really nice and you can't feel the lining."

"You know, I did some research on your pants." Michael shrugged. I am beginning to hate these pants. He put down the book on the table. "The reason you don't feel the lining is the Feindnix skin is extremely thin and without being properly preserved it will rip, so to prevent the leather from ripping, the lining protects it from the human skin that will wear off the coating."

Skyler's eyes widened. "Why did you do research on my pants?"

"They are made of the skin of the most sacred animal on Cassiopeia. And there are Cassiopeians that live on Earth. I may not like them, but I don't want you to be hurt over fashion."

"Fashion is supposed to hurt." Skyler laughed. "If you ever wanted to borrow these, then you should've asked me."

Michael sighed. Does this guy even listen to what I say?

Once Skyler got the right pants setting they waited in the room for Kax to come by. Kax came in wearing one of her glitter tanks tops; it just covered her boobs and a bit of her lower back. She was also wearing skintight leather pants.

Skyler took one look at her and his pants became tight. He sat down on the bed and placed his hands on his lap.

Michael was blown away by her style and how she wore the sides of her hair up. She was one sexy cat.

Skyler grinned. "Wow, someone is dressed all fancy."

She shot him a smile. "What this? It might be new, but this is hardly my best outfit."

Skyler grabbed his pillow and hugged it.

Michael couldn't take his eyes off Kax. "Wow, you look gorgeous tonight, are you ready to get going?"

Kax shot Michael a smile. "Thank you, and I'm ready to get going whenever Skyler's ready."

Michael noticed Skyler still had the pillow on his lap. "Skyler, are you okay?"

Damn, this is not the time, go away, go away. Think unsexy thoughts think unsexy thoughts. Skyler blushed. "I'm fine."

Kax and Michael made their way to the door.

He waited a few more seconds then crossed the room and tapped Kax on the shoulder. "You ready to shake that booty off tonight?"

Kax turned and grinned. "Yup, and my booty is going to be rocking it on the dance floor."

Skyler grinned. "You know, this club has private rooms upstairs."

Kax laughed. "That's good to know for when I meet someone new tonight."

Skyler frowned at Kax's comment. Michael then headed off ahead of them. Kax noticed Michael was down the hall, so she rushed to catch up and Skyler followed.

# Chapter 31

Dawn was on the rise when they headed back from the club. At headquarters, security stopped them at the gates. The large security officer wearing black with yellow stripes on his arm approached the side of their vehicle. "Sir, I will need to see your identification and your passengers," he told Michael.

They all pulled out their ID cards and handed them to Michael who showed them to the officer. "What is going? Is this a new thing, checking IDs?"

The officer scanned the ID cards, then handed them back. "Sir, do you know what just happened here?"

Michael shook his head. "Something happened? We were out all night, we didn't hear anything."

The officer sighed. "There was an attack. Some buildings have been damaged and right now security is really tight, so keep the IDs on you at all times."

Worried about the base, Skyler leaned over and appraised the officer. "Sir, what buildings were hit and was anyone hurt?"

The officer replied, "There were a few casualties. The hospital is full and only building 3A and 6G were hit, but last I heard, they captured the guys who did it."

Michael noticed he was getting a message from Dr. Kelley about his dad's condition. He asked the officer, "Are we done here, because my dad's in the hospital and…"

The officer cut him off. "Yes, you can go."

They rode into the base and instantly saw the damage. Michael dropped off Kax and Skyler at the door of the barracks and hurried to the hospital.

***

Skyler yawned and peered at Kax. "It seems like everything is under control. You want to get some sleep before class?"

Kax surveyed all the debris and broken buildings and yawned. "I guess we can get some sleep, I just can't believe the damage. There is so much. I wish I would have been here, I could have done something."

Skyler shook his head. "No, we couldn't have. We can't always save the day. Good thing is they caught the people. Feel good we didn't get hurt."

"I guess you're right."

Skyler gave her a drunk and tired hug. He waved goodbye and headed to his dorm.

Kax was surprised that it was all he did. She went up the stairs and to her dorm room. She had some trouble sleeping with all the worry, but soon found herself knocked out from exhaustion.

Chapter 32

Skyler awoke to the sound of someone in the room. He covered his head with a pillow to block the noise and spoke with a muffled voice, "What the heck is that noise? Stop, my head hurts."

Michael was packing up the room. He turned to Skyler. "I know you had a wild night but, really, do you plan to spend the remainder of the year in my bed naked with a hangover?"

Skyler examined himself and then scanned the room. "I must have passed out here. What, am I the first naked person in your bed? Why are you packing?"

Michael rolled his eyes and groaned. "I guess you are. You're lucky we don't have class today because of the attack. And I'm not staying here over the summer, so I thought I would get packing now."

Skyler took a few of Michael's pills and then sat up. "Dude, there are two weeks left. You don't have to pack up now that's what the last week of school is for."

Michael sighed. "I can't. My dad is not well. He was injured really badly. I am going to be taking my exams early so I can finish early and I won't be here during the summer or much over the next two weeks."

Skyler got off the bed putting on his pants and hugged Michael. "But what am I going to do without you? I'm stuck here for the summer. I was accepted into the summer program."

Michael shoved Skyler off and then checked down at his feet. "Sorry, I've got to get going. I won't see you until the fall. Hope you like your new roommate."

Skyler didn't want to lose Michael. Over the past seven months, Michael had started to grow on him. "You're not leaving today, are you? How about you just take some painkillers and lay down? You need some rest. I bet you haven't gotten any."

Michael shook his head and continued to pack. "I know I'm not leaving today, but my lack of sleep is not affecting my abilities to make decisions."

Skyler was worried about his roommate for a change and Michael's rash decision-making. What could he do to stop him? He thought about this as he watched Michael pack. "I guess it's a good thing you're not going into the summer program, then you don't have to worry about graduating sooner."

Michael sighed. "Good. I'll be glad, because I will not be a stupid engineer in this war. I am sick of these attacks. If we don't fight back, they will destroy everything on this planet."

Skyler found his clothes and began to get dressed. "So what is it you're afraid of?"

Michael turned his head and frowned at him. "I don't fear my death. Others, yes, but in my experience and my father's there aren't that many good captains right now. In our fathers' generation, captains were good, but it's been fifteen years and a whole new set. Few know how to fight in a war. You're lucky you get to choose what ship you're on or get to apply for a transfer. Not me. I'm a Squallite, so I don't, I go where they assign me. If I don't like it, it can be months to have them consider a transfer."

"That is so not fair. When I become captain, I will make sure you're on my ship." He finished putting on his clothes.

Michael shook his head. "If that's so, I'm going to volunteer for the war now."

Skyler's jaw dropped and he grabbed his chest. "Trust me, I have been doing the simulator tests, and I haven't lost a crewman yet."

Michael shook his head and kept on packing. "Simulations mean nothing. Life isn't simulated. You might be a good captain on screen, but who knows how you will be in real life?"

Skyler went over to Michael, closed his suitcase with his foot, and kicked the case under the bed.

Michael glared at him with his bloodshot eyes.

"Get some sleep before you say anything you will regret."

Michael stopped glaring and conceded. He got undressed and got into bed.

Skyler watched him. "I'll leave you alone for a bit and come back when you're sleeping." He left the room and headed off down the hall. He looked down the hall of the academy pondering which way he wanted to go. The girls' wing is just over there. I should go and check on Kax. Walking to the dorm, he saw a familiar face and smiled. She tossed her long black hair back. It was the girl from last night. They moved towards each other. "Hey, I didn't know you were a cadet?"

She flashed him a smile. "Yup, fifth year security. It's nice to see you again. Um, what's your name?"

He laughed. "Skyler Therris, and yours is?"

She flashed her eyes. "Roxanne Smith. So you're in the command division?"

"Yup, first year command cadet."

She traced her hand up and down his chest. "Hey, I know this is sudden, but you interested in going for some afternoon drinks?"

Skyler flashed his smile. "Sounds like a date."

Chapter 33

Kax went to the boys' room to see what everyone was doing. When no one answered, she used the key they gave her. All the lights were off and she peeked in to see Michael sleeping. She turned back to leave.

"Hey, Kax, is that you?" Michael opened his eyes.

She halted. "Yes, Michael, please go back to sleep. I didn't mean to wake you."

He smiled. "It's okay. What time is it?"

Kax looked at the clock on Skyler's side of the room. "Six p.m. I thought I would see what you're doing, but I didn't want to wake you."

Michael smiled. "I'm awake now and not because of you."

She smiled. "That's good to know, guess I will stay then." She switched on the light and sat on Skyler's bed.

Michael got out of bed and dressed. He sat back on his bed.

"So how is your dad doing?"

Michael answered, "Not well. Going to take the summer off to take care of him."

Kax's smiled faded. "So I won't see you until September, I guess. That's going to suck, I will miss you."

Michael shrugged. "There are still weekends?"

Kax shifted her head. "No, there isn't. I got accepted on a real pilot training mission, so I'm going to be on Andromeda Six all summer."

Michael frowned. "The space station. How did you manage that?"

Kax was proud of herself. "Skyler. On the last attack, he got me to pilot a ship, remember? Captain Hart recommended me for the mission. Don't tell Skyler, or he will be jealous."

"Captain Hart is with Fleet Admiral Davis. Does that mean you're going to switch fleets too?"

Kax shook her head. "No, not yet. Any cadet can get the mission, because it's summer, but once the fall comes, if I still want to study under Captain Hart, I will have to switch. No plans to do that yet."

"I wish you the best. I think Skyler is stuck on Earth."

Kax sighed. "Year's almost over. Only exams left. Once they are done, we will all part ways."

Michael nodded. "Remember to e-mail me, that's all I ask."

"It's a deal."

***

Skyler then came running into the room and closed the door. Michael and Kax regarded him strangely.

Michael frowned. "Why are you running? One of your girl's boyfriends see you?"

Skyler was trying to catch his breath. "Worse, there's a lockdown. The Cassiopeians are in the building. I saw them, and they are armed. This is serious."

The alarms in the halls started clanging.

Michael checked out the window. "This is not a couple of them. This is an invasion." He closed the blinds, and they hid under Michael's bed.

Kax huddled between the two boys. "What are we going to do?"

Skyler tried to think. "I have no idea. This is bad and, for once, I'm out of ideas."

Michael paused. "I have an idea. They locked down the school, but they don't lock down the vents, so we take the vent out of this room and make our way to the armory."

Kax's eyes filled with worry. "You don't think we can actually fight these things, do you?"

Michael sighed. "It's almost 10 p.m., and the place is locked down. What do you think is going to happen if we stay here?"

Skyler spoke up. "Stay alive?"

Michael snapped back. "No! I saw their ship out there. They're here for business. Call the fleet admiral and warn him in case he doesn't know. We're going to fight."

Skyler and Kax exchanged glances. They had no idea how they were going to do it, but they would at least try.

Michael snuck over to Skyler's bed, hoping not to be seen through the window, and opened the vent. He told the others, "Okay, come on up. We have to be very quiet."

"That vent is so small, how are we going to fit and how can you be quiet in a vent? Haven't you heard of an echo?" Kax blurted out, trembling. Skyler wrapped his arm around her.

Michael paused. "Move very slowly and get in. Try not to make any noise."

Skyler crawled out from under the bed with Kax. "How do you know that this vent goes to the armory?"

"This one doesn't. This will take you to the back of the building. We can climb to the outside of the building and from there, sneak across the field, where I will change the wires on the armory to give us about thirty seconds to get in, get our weapons and get out."

"That's a stupid idea. Now we have no weapons, and what if the Cass attack us? And thirty seconds isn't long enough to load up with weapons."

There was a knock at the door.

"Who is it?" Skyler called.

Michael covered his face and whispered, "You don't ask that when there is an intruder. It could be them."

Skyler crept quietly over to the door and slowly inched it open. Michael jumped off the bed, ready to defend them. Their hearts dropped and their eyes widened when they saw Fleet Admiral Cane.

The fleet admiral closed the door. He came deeper into the room. "You three aren't going anywhere. I know you three like to get into trouble when things like this happen. But this is not the time to do it. We were ready for this attack, so special forces are in the works. In case the intruders come, I brought you these."

He opened his jacket to reveal four fusion ray guns. He gave one to each of them and then put the fourth one on his belt.

Skyler looked at his and pretended to fire.

Cane frowned. "Don't do that, these can kill you. They are set on low, but can still kill."

The other two kept them at their sides.

Michael spoke up. "So, you want us to sit around while armed and wait for them to get us?"

Cane nodded. "Kind of, they are after me. They know I am one of the three heads and I know you three love to play hero so where better to hide out? Davis is hiding and Thompson is off planet. We have to be quiet though. They could walk by and hear us at any time."

Michael got up on the bed and closed the vent. "You're right, Admiral. We will take a watch and sleep in shifts."

The fleet admiral shook his head. "We don't have to go to that extreme. I just don't want to make too much noise."

"So, can we play games? Or do you want to tell stories? We have to kill time somehow." Skyler was eager to start his adventure.

Kax spoke up. "Ya, I want to ask a question. If my mother was the pilot for Skyler's father, are me and him brother and sister?"

All three men stared at her. Cane chuckled. "No. That's the short answer. You're a year apart and your mom wasn't our pilot when you were born."

Skyler looked over at Kax. "How did you know about this? And no, you're not my sister. I don't have a sister."

Michael cut in. "Fleet Admiral Cane told us about how you knew him when you were in jail."

All eyes were on Fleet Admiral Cane.

He sat down on the edge of the bed. "Okay, I'll start at the beginning. I wanted to be captain one day, but I couldn't get a promotion. I didn't have enough experience, they said. That's when I met your father. They assigned me to his crew saying it would be a good way to gain experience faster, they were right. I was so jealous that he was a few years younger and he got to be a captain, but I had rushed my way through the academy. It wasn't long before we became friends..."

There was a loud bang that came from down the hall.

Cane jumped to his feet. "Michael, check the door."

Michael poked his head out of the room. "I don't see anything. I think it was above us."

"Thank you, Michael. Please stay near the door and keep an eye on things. Kax, watch the window, and Skyler, keep an eye on that vent," Cane ordered.

All of them got to their posts and waited with weapons in hand.

"While we wait, let me continue the story." Cane sat with his gun in his lap. "Skyler's father met your mother soon after. I liked her too, but she wanted your father more. Then they got married and had Skyler. We had a pilot, and he was nice to talk to but he wasn't a good pilot. We put up with him until one day he flew us too close to the sun and almost killed us all..."

There was another crash and screams coming from above them.

"Shouldn't we do something? Those people sound like they have been hurt." Kax snapped.

Cane shook his head. "No. Your job is to make sure I don't get killed. Forces would be in chaos if they lost a fleet admiral. There are others out there fighting them off."

Skyler jumped down from the bed, "Kax. Let's trade spots. My legs are hurting from standing on this mattress."

"Sounds good to me." Kax got on the bed and Skyler went to the window.

"I'll talk quieter, but they shouldn't suspect me to be in here." Cane continued with the story. "So we got a new pilot, Karmantha, Kax's mother. She was as lovely as she was smart. Kax, you were already born by this time. But with one problem solved, another arose. Sandy, Skyler's mother, wanted to raise him on earth and so she refused to go back into space. She regretted that once she met Karma. While Sandy was on Earth, Captain Therris fell madly in love with Karma. The two of them bonded over the fact that they missed their families and that their spouses didn't understand space like they did."

There was a loud knock at the door.

Michael whispered. "Cane, were you expecting anyone?"

Cane covered his mouth with his finger.

"Ahh!" Skyler screamed. He pushed the blind over to reveal a nasty long horned and toothed scar faced Cassiopeian glaring back at them.

Cane jumped behind the end board and ducked for cover.

Michael jerked around and shot at the window. The laser bunched off the window and hit Skyler's pillow.

"They're bullet proof!" Kax shouted.

"Hey! That was my pillow!" Skyler snapped.

There was another knock at the door. A hissing voice came from the other side. "We knows there's Ssomeone on the other Sside of thiss doors. Comes out with yours handss up."

Skyler aimed his gun towards the door. "We're going down fighting."

They all nodded in agreement.

The Cassiopeian soldiers blasted the door lock, and the door swung open.

Skyler and Michael began taking shots at the Cassiopeian soldiers. Kax joined in on the fight.

Cane hid in the closet with the gun ready to fire.

They knocked the three Cassiopeians to the ground. Skyler and Michael moved their bodies out into the hall and closed the door on their way back in.

"What about the lock on the door?" Kax asked.

"I will take the laser gun apart and weld it shut," Michael said.

"But how do we get out?" Skyler added.

"A blast broke it, and a blast will break it again. If not, we have a window and a vent to exit out of."

Cane stepped out of the closet. "I hope you all realize I am not normally this cowardly but..."

"They are trying to kill you, we understand, Cane," Michael responded.

"Would anyone like me to finish my story?" Cane asked.

Michael nodded and barded the door. "I would love to hear the rest. I still have a few questions."

Cane sat back down on the bed. "About two years later, the darkest day in the United Galactic Forces' history came. We were returning from a trade mission when for no reason, we were attacked. Your father did the best job of his life to try to save us all. What couldn't be transported down was sent in escape pods. Everyone on the ship except your father made it. He died the greatest hero of them all."

A tear glimmered in Cane's eye. "Skyler, I was the one who told your mother. She was so upset, and you were so little. I was there for you as a child. I tried to be there when you got older. I was willing to give it all up to make sure you had a good life but Sandy didn't want me around and without notice she married your stepfather Charles…"

Skyler sat next to Cane on the bed. "I appreciate all you did do."

Cane let out a deep sigh. "I am sorry. I tried to stay in touch."

He peered over at Kax. "Kax, I did stay in contact with your mother, but she was happy in her life and she died in the line of duty three years later. Pirates invaded her ship, and she was shot along with the rest of the crew. Horrible way for anyone to go. I miss her and the old crew so much. It's nice to see you guys all together as friends, your parents would have wanted it like that."

Their faces were long.

Michael asked the fleet admiral, "So, what about my dad? How do you know him?"

Cane smiled. "He was our backup mechanic. He never went to space with us, but there were a few times when our mechanics weren't around and we had to grab whoever was around. Your father was and still is great at his job. Everything he fixes never breaks."

Michael smiled. "That sounds like my dad. You wouldn't happen to know who my mother is, would you?"

Cane shook his head. "I'm sorry, I didn't know your dad back then, and if I remember correctly, I think he joined United Galactic Forces after you were born. Don't quote me on it, but I think that's right."

A look of disappointment came over Michael's face.

"Don't let that story get you down it was a long time ago." Cane examined the door and suggested, "I don't think we're going to be seeing anymore intruders for the night and no going sleeping after all that. How about we play game of Holo-Monopoly?"

They all smiled and agreed. Skyler pulled out his tablet and brought up a new game and they played on and on into the night.

***

In the morning, they all woke. The intruders were gone and the fleet admiral was preparing to leave.

Skyler got out of his bed. "Thank you, Admiral, for coming it was a good night."

Cane patted Skyler on the back. "I hope I answered all your questions last night."

"You sure did, Blinky."

Cane ruffled Skyler's hair. "You have earned the right to call me that." He winked with his one non-patched eye. "You kids have a nice summer and see you back here next year, and no goofing off."

They all heard the fleet admiral's message and nodded their heads.

"Thank you, Cane, for a great year," Michael got out of his bed and stood at attention.

"No, thank you. I was glad to see you all together. I'm happy you joined United Galactic Forces. With you on our side, there will not be a war."

Kax got out of bed and gave Cane a hug, "Good luck and thank you for everything."

He hugged Kax back, "Your mother would be so proud of you." He broke the hug and went to Skyler giving him one last hug.

"Never stop chasing those stars." He whispered into Skyler's ear before he left the room.

Who knew what the summer would bring? Their journey was just starting.

# ACKNOWLEDGEMENT

I would like to thank my editor Stacy Juba for all her hard work. My friends Leah Keeler, Kandice Saur, Oliver Brackenbury and Sharon Lipman for helping me the small but major things. Thank you to my parents for the financial support needed in getting this book to print.
Anyone else who has listened to me ramble or has had any input. You have all helped in making this book what it is.

www.ingramcontent.com/pod-product-compliance
Lightning Source LLC
Chambersburg PA
CBHW062139170626
46813CB00002B/754